CW00434064

ADORABLE FAT GIRL
TAKES UP YOGA

By Bernice Bloom

Published internationally by Gold Medals Media Ltd:

© Bernice Bloom 2018

Terms and Conditions:
The purchaser of this book is subject to the condition that he/she shall in no way resell it, nor any part of it, nor make copies of it to distribute freely.

All Persons Fictitious Disclaimer:
This book is a work of fiction. Any similarity between the characters within its pages and persons, living or dead, is unintentional and coincidental.

* * *

CONTENTS

CHAPTER ONE

"Oh Charlie, I don't know what to do," I said. "My life's falling apart."

I was standing in my friend's doorway, clutching a bottle of wine and wearing a look of dismay and disbelief.

"Oh blimey, what's happened?" she asked, ushering me inside. "Nice tan, by the way."

"That's kind of the problem," I attempted to explain.

"What? The tan is the problem? Doesn't look like much of a problem to me. Wine?"

"Yes please." I followed Charlie through to the kitchen while I explained that I had the lovely tan because I'd just been on a three-week cruise. That same cruise had led to me putting on 10lbs. Ten bloody pounds. If I told you that I went on the cruise weighing 19 stone and 6lbs, and came back weighing 20 stone and 2lbs, you may get some measure of the problem. I had crossed the 20-stone barrier. A hugely significant mental as well as physical weight. I couldn't believe it. TWENTY stone! Don't tell anyone. I was ashamed and completely devastated.

I usually laughed and joked to hide my embarrassment but I was genuinely very concerned about this recent development.

I had been doing so well with my weight loss until the cruise. I went to Fat Club at the beginning of the year and lost a stone and a half. I felt amazing, reinvigorated and wonderful. I thought about what I was eating, I began walking instead of getting the bus whenever possible and the pounds dropped off. But then I started to get a bit bored of it all, and found I was eating more which then led to me not caring as much, and the weight piled on. Now

I had crossed the 20-stone mark and I felt devastated.

Charlie sighed and shook her head. "Well, you'll have to cut back, won't you," she said.

"Cutting back is for someone who's a couple of pounds over fighting weight, not for someone who weighs more than a mini metro," I said.

"You don't weigh more than a car," she replied. "Cars are really heavy."

"I'M really heavy," I responded.

"You need to do some exercise," she said. "Come and join me on my training runs."

"Mate, you're training for a half marathon. I can't walk across the room without panting like a chain-smoking pensioner. Running with you is going to end up with me in an ambulance on the way to a lung transplant."

"You should try one of the classes at my gym, you might like those...there are loads and loads of them," said Charlie.

"Like what?"

"Well – there is Zumba?" she suggested.

"What on earth is that? Zumba sounds like the name of the leader of a Nigerian tribe, not an exercise class."

"It's a dance class. Look..." she reached for her laptop and called up 'Zumba'.

Loud music burst out through her computer as energised, young, fit women in various shades of brightly coloured lycra danced, pranced and jumped around on the screen while a wildly enthusiastic instructor shouted at them. They just kept moving, dancing and spinning, hollering and shrieking. They seemed much slimmer and fitter than I was.

"I would rather sit there with a Stanley knife cutting the fat of my body," I said to Charlie. "Is this an American thing...this Zumba business? I can't imagine anyone with British blood doing it."

"It's great fun, the classes are always packed out," said Charlie. "You should try these things, they might look scary on the screen, but when you're there and the loud music is playing, you'll find you really enjoy it and get fit without realising you're exercising."

"We both know that is a complete lie. Are there any other exercise classes?"

"Yes, there are the traditional classes like aerobics and step."

"No," I said before she had barely finished the sentence. "I tried those when I was 10 stone lighter and hated them. Step is just ridiculous. Thirty fully grown women stepping on and off a bit of plastic that's been put in front of them to trip them up. No thank you. Anything else?"

"Maybe aquarobics will be for you?" said Charlie. "It's a gentler exercise. You don't have any idea how hard you're working at the time because the water supports you, but you definitely feel it the next day. Also, you are in water so you won't get injured or anything. It might be a nice introduction to getting back into exercise."

That did, indeed, sound like a rather nice way to lose the weight.

"Call it up," I said to Charlie, and she keyed aquarobics into Google and called up a video of a class.

Now maybe I was being overly fussy, but the image that greeted me, of ageing ladies in swim caps waving their arms in the air while a tinny version of Madonna's *Into the Groove* screeched in the background, didn't seem like a wholly worthwhile use of anyone's time.

"Is this a class for old people?" I asked.

"Well it's a gentle exercise class, as I said, so obviously it's bound to attract older people, but you get young people doing it too, and it is, genuinely, a tough workout. "

I looked again at the women in their swim hats...wrinkly faces looking out from beneath flowery plastic headgear. I didn't think it was for me.

"Anything else?" I ventured, realising that Charlie was going to get pretty fed up very soon.

"I don't know...there are spin classes, but they are really hard-core, you sit on a bike for an hour cycling furiously, sweat flying everywhere, I don't think you'd like them."

"Nope, that doesn't sound like my sort of thing at all."

"What do you think is your sort of thing?" Charlie asked.

"Lying on my back and pointing my toes occasionally?" I suggested.

"I know!" shrieked Charlie all of a sudden. "I know what you should do to get yourself back into exercising slowly."

"And this involves lying on your back pointing your toes occasionally?" I said.

"Pretty much," said Charlie, tapping away into Google. Onto the screen sprang a lovely image of lots of people lying down while the instructor told them to breathe in deeply and then breathe out again... Breathe in, and breathe out again. I could do that!

"This looks perfect," I said. "What the hell is it?"

"Why," said Charlie with a flourish. "This, my dear friend, is yoga."

On the screen they continued to lie there while the instructor issued gentle commands about breathing and stretching. All of the women looked super slim and toned and happy and deeply relaxed while the lovely instructor talked kindly to them.

"Where do I sign up?" I asked Charlie. "I want to be a yoga lady."

CHAPTER TWO

At work the next day I couldn't stop thinking about our conversation. The more I thought about yoga, the more it seemed to me like it would be the answer to all my woes. One session of lying on the floor in attractive yoga pants and a funky t shirt would act as a panacea - somehow transforming me...through osmosis or something...into a beautiful, slim and lovely woman who was relaxed, flexible and serene at all times. The more we'd sat there last night, watching videos while eating crisps and drinking wine, the more converted I'd become to life as a yogi. It seemed like the key to body transformation. A bit of chanting, some toe touching and a new leotard and I, too, would look like those wondrous women in the videos. I could hardly contain my new-found enthusiasm for the world. The only mystery was why on earth I hadn't done this years ago.

I had memorised some of the poses they'd done in the class on YouTube, and as I watered the geraniums in the garden centre (I work here, I'm not just randomly going around garden centres watering the plants or anything), I tried to think of the poses I'd seen. There was the downward dog which was pretty much the position I ended up in whenever I tried to pick something up off the floor when I was drunk. It's one thing bending over when you're drunk and slim, quite another thing bending over when you're drunk and 20 stone.

The women in the video had done things like headstands and bridges which I knew would be entirely beyond me. It would take a crane to get me up there and 20 highly qualified medical professionals to get me safely down afterwards.

Then there were positions that I probably couldn't do at the moment but, with a little instruction and some concerted effort, I thought I'd probably be able to do at some stage. One of those was the tree pose. For all you yoga virgins out there, this is when you stand on one leg and put the sole of your other foot on the inside thigh of the leg you are standing on. You start by putting the foot on the inside of your calf, then knee, then inner thigh as you progress then – ta da! – you have your foot flat on the inside of your thigh, right at the top, and you are doing tree pose.

I looked up...no one was around, so I put down the watering can and decided to give tree pose a go. I balanced on one foot...not all that simple when you're a larger lady and attempted to place a foot onto my inner calf. Gosh, much harder than it looked.

I moved nearer to the wall so I could reach out and hold on if I felt myself falling. I tried again. I stood up straight and tried to ground myself, then I slowly lifted my right leg, and attempted to put my foot on the inside of my calf. It was hopeless. I felt myself fall as soon as I took one foot off the ground. How could I be so unbalanced?

Right, one more try...I lifted my leg really slowly and, trying to ignore the wobbling, put the sole of my shoe onto the inside of my calf. I lasted about a second before I felt myself start to fall. I moved my arms around to try and balance myself but it was no good, I pitched to the side and reached up quickly, intending to lean on the wall, but I was falling faster than I realised so I made a grab for the nearest thing - a luscious, flower-filled hanging basket that Maureen had spent all morning designing and planting.

I went flying to the ground, one arm wind milling furiously, the other one still clinging to the basket. I hit the ground first and the basket came crashing down on top of me - mud and pansies everywhere and me in the middle, lying on my back.

I wiped the dirt out of my eyes and looked up...there was Keith, my boss, along with Sandra from indoor plants and Jerry from the carpentry section. They were all struggling not to laugh.

"Are you OK?" asked Keith, while the other two bit their lips and choked back their amusement at my plight.

"Yes, I'm fine," I said. "Absolutely fine. I just tripped on some dirt. People need to make sure they clean up after themselves. Someone could really hurt themselves when there's dirt lying around." I wiped the mud off my face and lifted the lovely little flowers off my uniform.

"What were you doing?" asked Jess.

"Just watering the plants," I said.

"We were watching you on the cctv cameras in our break," said Jerry. "Were you trying to be a flamingo or something? You kept standing on one leg, it was very weird."

"If you must know, I was practising yoga," I said, rolling over and clambering onto my feet. "That move I was doing was called the tree pose."

"Oh," they said, simultaneously. And Keith added: "Well, as long as you're OK. We need to get on, Jerry."

The two of them wandered off, laughing, and leaving me with Jess.

"Do you do much yoga?" she asked.

"I do," I replied. "And I'm going to be doing much more in the future. Though not at work, obviously."

"No, best not destroy any more hanging baskets," said Jess, crouching down to collect the flowers that were strewn all around. "My friend is brilliant at yoga. She's really strong and flexible and says 'Namaste' all the time."

"Yes, like me," I said, nodding as I spoke.

"I think it's amazing that you do yoga. Good for you. Shall I stay and help you clear all this up?" she asked.

"No, it's fine. I can do it. Thanks Jess. And – Namaste."

"Namaste to you too," she replied.

CHAPTER THREE

Charlie rang at lunchtime.

"Slight problem," she said.

"Namaste," I replied.

"What? Anyway, I've been looking at yoga classes at my gym and you have to do the beginners' course first, before you're allowed to go to the normal, timetabled classes."

"Oh, OK, I'll do that then," I replied. "To be honest, a beginners' course wouldn't be a bad idea, I have a feeling it's harder than it looks." I omitted to tell her that my initial experiences with tree pose had left me covered in mud and pansies, and the laughing stock of the shop. I still had soil down the front of my uniform but she didn't need to know about that.

"Yes - I agree. The trouble is - the next course is in September, two months away, and it's already fully booked and with a six-person waiting list. The course after that is in February. Shall I book us onto the February one?"

"No," I yelled. "I don't want to wait til then. It's July now. I planned to be eight stone for Christmas. Is there anything else we can do? I want to learn how to do the tree pose."

"The tree pose? Really? OK, well, there are a few options...we could go to a different gym, join up there, and see whether we could do a yoga course at that gym, but all the other gyms in the area are really expensive."

"Yeah, I'm not all that fond of doing anything really expensive, and you want to stay at Palisades while you're doing your marathon training, don't you?"

"Yes, ideally," replied Charlie. "There is something else we could do though. We could go on a yoga retreat where they teach you all the basics, then when we come back we could go along to lessons and tell them we've done a beginners' course, so they'd let us straight on. That would be much quicker."

"That sounds good," I said. "Kind of yoga cramming for the weekend."

"Yeah, I think so," said Charlie. "There's a course this weekend at a place called Vishraam House in the New Forest. Two nights stay...beginners' yoga."

"Let's do it," I said boldly. "Come on, let's get ourselves onto this course and into lycra."

"Maybe I should come around to yours tonight and we'll look through it properly, then book it if you think you fancy it. You know – if you think you're up to it."

"Up to it? I think yoga is going to be the making of me," I said. "Just you wait."

Charlie came around at 7pm that evening and I had to unravel myself before I could answer the door. I was trying the tree pose again, but this time I was using a pair of tights to lift my foot into place while leaning against the wall. Even with the help of the prop it was proving quite a task. My hands were sore from pulling on the tights and my foot wouldn't go into place.

"Come in," I said, still with tights in hand. Charlie gave me a book about yoga. "For you," she said. "Keep it on your bedside table." She glanced at the underwear in my hand but I couldn't summon the words to explain, so I sat her down and began the process of finding out about yoga weekends.

"Show me the retreats then," I said, and I thought how grown up Charlie and I seemed looking at the images of health, fitness and good living on the screen. All the holidays we'd ever been on before had resulted in hospital visits, altercations with the police, and huge amounts of drinking. This time it would be altogether different.

"Here we are," she said. "Look - there are various different types of courses...you can specialise in different yogas...there's Ashtanga - isn't that the one that Madonna does? And I think Hatha yoga is the Megan Markle one. I don't know which one is better? And what's this Bikram Yoga? Hang on, isn't that the one that Pippa Middleton does?"

"I don't know," I said as I looked down the list...there were so many. "Aerial yoga? What the hell is that?" I asked. Charlie shrugged. We didn't really know what we were doing at all.

"Look up aerial yoga, I have to know," I commanded. For some reason, when it came to any sort of research or planning, it was always Charlie sitting in front of the screen, and me barking orders.

"Oh blimey. Very 50 shades of grey," she said, turning the screen round so I could see. There were lots of people hanging from the ceiling by ropes, with little hammocks at the bottom. They were pulling themselves up the ropes and rolling out of the hammocks. It looked fraught with danger. If the thing took my weight in the first place it was sure to be impossible for me to get in and out of it.

"Na," I said, and she nodded in agreement.

"Oh, how about one of these?" she said. She had pulled up a list of general yoga courses where you did all the different yogas on one weekend, instead of having to specialise...they came in beginners, intermediate and advanced.

"Here we go," said Charlie. "A basic introduction to all the different types of yoga as well as meditation, mindfulness and clean living."

"Sounds like us," I said. "Oh, but how about this one?"

Below it were the more advanced courses including one called 'guru-led advanced course.' "Stick it in the basket. I want a guru," I said, clicking on it and adding it into out virtual shopping bag.

"Oy, stop it. I don't think either of us is ready for an advanced course," said Charlie.

"OK - gurus next time," I conceded, and we booked ourselves onto a beginners' course for the weekend by emailing a woman called Venetta.

"I'm quite excited," I said. "It's run by someone whose name sounds a little bit like an ice-cream...that has to be a good thing, surely."

"Definitely," she agreed, with a small squeal. "This could be really good fun. I hope I don't make a fool of myself."

"Oh, come now, Charlie," I replied. "We both know which one of us is more likely to make a fool of herself."

CHAPTER FOUR

In the lead up to the course, I thought it would be wise to try and start living the life that I would be required to live on the retreat. I couldn't go from full-blown Chinese takeaways and large glasses of sauvignon to slices of air dried mango, chakras and finding your inner goddess. I needed to ease myself into the new lifestyle gently, so I vowed to try and eat as healthily as possible in the few days before we left.

I started making changes on the Thursday morning, the day before departure. I had a mug of hot water with a squeeze of lemon in it. It was supposed to curb my appetite and take away the hunger for a fried breakfast and loads of mid-morning biscuits. It tasted so awful, though, I could barely drink the stuff. I only had a couple of sips and knew that if I were to have any chance of finishing it I'd have to add sugar which would completely spoil the whole point of doing it in the first place.

Instead I sipped green tea and ate slices of apple. Christ it was dull. I phoned Charlie.

"This is shit, isn't it?" I said, looking at the limp pieces of peeled apple lying pathetically on the plate in front of me.

"Yep," she said. "But just imagine - we'll get used to healthy eating and come back completely transformed. Just try to keep going...it'll do you the world of good. I'm about to have some grapefruit."

"Ahhh..." I said. "That's the evillest of all the fruits. To be honest, I don't know how it has the audacity to call itself a fruit. It's awful stuff."

The whole day was ruined by the thought, lingering in my head, that I wasn't allowed to have anything nice to eat, and that I would be hungry all the time. My breaks weren't any fun and lunchtime was pointless. Chicken salad? I mean - what's the point? Where's the warmth, happiness or joy to be derived from chewy poached chicken and a collection of garden leaves?

I got home that evening and slumped on the sofa, feeling out of sorts and slightly angry with the world. Ted, my boyfriend, was due to be coming around for the evening because I wouldn't see him for the next few days, but I couldn't face company, I felt all empty inside. I'm not sure whether anyone who doesn't overeat could ever understand this, but without being able to eat food that filled me up and made me feel all warm and lovely inside, I felt horrible. All irritable and like there was no point to anything. The whole world felt prickly. I was unbalanced and cross. I told Ted that I had a headache and sat on the sofa to spend the evening feeling sorry for myself.

I know this probably sounds pathetic, but it was just so horrible being hungry. I felt so deprived, and that led to feelings of loneliness and sadness. Lack of food seemed to signal lack of comfort and warmth. I started to think that my life was not worth living...in my mind I began to question my job, my boyfriend, my friends and my family.

Eating isn't just about putting food inside me, it's about nurturing, warming and comforting myself and stopping myself from feeling sad and lonely. And - I know what you're thinking - I should address the things that were making me feel sad and lonely rather than just eating myself into an emotional slumber but doing that would take months of self-analysis and confrontation with my darkest fears. Whereas a cheeky chicken and black bean sauce would take half an hour to arrive and I'd feel great. That's why - at the end of the day - whenever I felt low, I always ate.

And it was very easy for me to justify overeating to myself. When I couldn't think of anything else but being full of lovely, tasty food, I could easily convince myself that eating obscene amounts was actually the best thing I could possibly do.

On that warm evening, I picked up the takeaway leaflet and told myself that this was the last chance I had to eat a big meal, and it would actually be a good thing if I ate well tonight because it would make me more committed and give me the strength to really throw myself into the weekend ahead.

So, I ordered the food, and felt almost drunk and helpless with anticipation while I waited for it to arrive. The ring on the bell sent electric pulses of joy through me and I practically danced to the door to collect the food. I had chicken and black bean sauce with egg fried rice and chips and seaweed, and I ate all the free prawn crackers that came with it. I loved eating when there was a lot of food. When I started picking at the food and could see there was absolutely loads more to eat, it gave me a real thrill.

The food was not quite the same without a couple of glasses of wine, of course, so I did that too. Knocking back the white wine while I ate a big plateful. After my first round, there was still a tonne of food left, so then I lay back on the sofa and picked at the rest of it with my hands, dipping chips into the remaining drops of black bean sauce and pushing handfuls of seaweed into my mouth. I'm like an animal when I eat. It's always better that I'm alone when I get the real hungers. I poured myself another large glass of wine, feeling drunk on food and alcohol and completely relaxed, like I'd just had that drug you have before an anaesthetic...the one that knocks you out a bit and makes you feel drowsy without rendering you completely unconscious.

I felt so lovely. There were crumbs all over the place and I'd managed to get dribbles of black bean sauce on my sweatshirt, but that didn't matter, they could be cleaned. All that mattered was that I felt relaxed and happy and lovely. I just wanted to lay there and bask in the loveliness for a while. I knew I'd feel rotten later...really low and disappointed in myself and frustrated at my lack of any kind of willpower, but I'd deal with those feelings when they arose. For now, it was all about the feelings of light-headedness, satisfaction and warmth. Mmmm...

When I woke the next morning the memory of what I'd done hit me in an instant. Shit, I'd had a huge takeaway and a bottle of wine the night before. Damn. I'd bought lemons and apples and all sorts of healthy food so that I wouldn't be tempted over to the dark side, then I'd gone and bloody ordered a takeaway. God. I'd just have to try and be really good this weekend to make up for it. I sat up in bed and saw the yoga book, perched on my bedside cabinet, waiting to be read.

I turned to the section by a woman called Rachel Brathen. In it, the woman was describing all sorts of thoroughly awful things that had happened to her when she was younger. She wrote about how she was drinking too much and being sick and how her life was totally out of control...then she found yoga, and everything came together for her. She felt peace at last. A lovely warm feeling ran through me as I read the words and absorbed her philosophy, I started to regret the colossal amount of food I'd just eaten.

"There is no need to change your habits to make space for a yoga practice," she wrote. "Start practising yoga from where you are today, and let the practice change you. The more often you come to the mat, on your own or in a class, the easier it will be to make healthy decisions throughout the rest of your day. When you're listening more to your body, you'll find that it's not as difficult to eat well. With awareness of your body you'll find it easier to stay away from sugar or alcohol or whatever it is that you're looking to remove from your diet. Or perhaps you will realise that the foods you're eating are just fine, nothing to obsess over at all! The bottom line is, you will be more conscious about how your body feels and how sensitive it is to what you put in it. May be that the second helping of food didn't make you feel better, after all.

"When we live more in the body and less in the mind, those choices that were so overwhelming before become easier to make. I know that when I really listen to my body, it very rarely wants two huge helpings of food. If I reach for more, it's probably because I'm busy talking and socialising or I'm feeling emotional. If I stay mindful, I'll be able to tell when I'm full. Much of what we eat in a day is simply a result of boredom. I'm not promising you'll stop wanting dessert or wine or all the good things that come with life just because you start practising yoga. You'll simply be more receptive to what your body wants and needs. And this is the very first step to healthy you."

I wished I hadn't eaten all that food last night. I wished I could think of other ways to cope when I was overcome by this emotional hunger that seemed to suck me into it, so that I had no control over myself. Sometimes the feeling was so overpowering that I felt I had no choice but to eat. Perhaps yoga could help me find a balance. Find peace?

CHAPTER FIVE

"I can't quite believe we're doing this, can you?" Charlie said, as I slid into the car next to her and made a token effort to put the seat belt on knowing there was no way on earth it would go around me. I squeezed and pulled and then dropped it, letting it fall down by my side. Luckily her's wasn't a bleeping seat belt. Those cars that start beeping at you when you can't do the seat belt up are a pain for anyone over about a size 20. I'm a size 26 these days. The damn car can bleep as much as it wants, the seat belt won't go around me however much noise it makes.

"I think this weekend might be good for us," I said. Charlie raised her eyebrows in amazement. "You know, I read the yoga book you gave me and it all sounded really great. This woman was writing about how much it had helped her, spiritually, and I thought - this weekend could be life changing. It could be the time I get myself sorted, get myself together and really clear my life out. You never know.

"Well let's hope so," said Charlie. "I can't say I'm feeling as positive. I hate being really hungry and I think they only give us tiny portions. I'm worried it's going to be really hard to concentrate on the yoga and do really well at it when we're hungry all the time."

"Well, yes, I'm not great with hunger either," I said. "I did treat myself to the most enormous takeaway last night."

"Whaaat? I thought we were trying to detox yesterday, so we'd be ready for today."

"I know, but I just couldn't. I feel so miserable when I'm hungry."

"You're gonna be great company at a bloody detox yoga weekend then, aren't you?"

We drove along in silence for a while.

"So, how much food do you think we'll get at this place?"

"I don't know, but all the comments on the website say that it was a great place except for that fact that they were all starving the whole time."

"Oh God, this is going to be horrible, isn't it? I'm dreading it now. I don't mind eating healthy foods, if we have to, but I don't want to be hungry. Should we get some snacks just in case it gets desperate?"

"We're supposed to be detoxing," said Charlie, admonishingly. "Maybe we should try and do it by eating their food, and see how we go?"

"Really?" I replied, looking over at Charlie. "OK, fine. If you think you can survive for three days on half a cashew nut and a teaspoon of peach extract, I'm sure I can too."

"Oh, sod it," she said, veering across two lanes of traffic and into the service station. "Let's get some nibbles so we have supplies in our bags in case things get desperate. Like you say, we don't have to eat them all, do we?"

"No, it will be useful to have them, just in case we want them."

"Yes."

We decided that I would be in charge of snack purchasing, so Charlie put petrol in while I went inside and filled up with low fat crisps, unsalted nuts, rice cakes and a couple of bottles of wine...just in case. Then I looked at the tragic selection of produce and thought again. There could be 20 people on this course...we could end up having midnight feasts. We really needed more than this. I put in a few grab bags of normal crisps, tortilla chips and tubes of pringles, I added more wine, biscuits, sweets and two whole cakes, walking to the check out and throwing in pork pies, sausage rolls and other meat treats. I was barely able to carry the basket. I put in scotch eggs and more crisps. It came to £70. Blimey! Still, if it meant that we could host a great pyjama party in our room, it would be worth every penny, and if we didn't we could easily bring it back with us. We didn't have to eat it all.

I got back to the car with my four shopping bags full of goodies. Charlie was in the shop paying for petrol. I plonked the bags in the boot and suddenly felt a bit daft; I'd got really carried away in the shop just then. We didn't need anything like this much food. I felt a bit stupid. Charlie would think I'd lost my mind. Luckily, I had a big suitcase with me with lots of room so I decanted all of the goodies I could fit into my case until there was just one bag left. It had low fat crisps, one bottle of wine, low fat sausage rolls and rice cakes in it. There. Charlie would think I'd been very sensible now, but I could roll out the rest of the food if there was any need for it. I shut the boot and got into the car.

"Right, where are we going?" Charlie asked, as she took her seat beside me.

"I don't know," I said. "You're holding the map."

"I can't drive and look at it, you'll have to read it."

"I'm rubbish at anything map-related," I said. "You know how rubbish at map reading I am. We'll end up in Norfolk."

"No, we won't, and we'll have the sat nav on, we just need to keep an eye on the map as well because the instructions from the centre say that it is quite hard to find."

"OK," I said.

"Did you not get any snacks in the end?" Charlie asked.

"Yep, just a couple of things. I put the bag in the boot," I said.

"Great. OK, let's go. The location is plugged into the sat nav, you have the map - we're sure to be OK."

I should point out that no one, in the history of the world, has ever said that me map reading would mean us being ok.

Still, Charlie seemed convinced and we settled into driving along the pretty country lanes, guided by the satnav. I sat back and relaxed, wallowing in the tranquil sights as we moved further away from home, and closer to our weekend rural retreat. The sun's rays reached through the windows as we drove along, caressing my face and arm. It was lovely.

"Right, this is where I could do with your help," said Charlie. I was half asleep, enjoying the gentle motion of the car when I was brought joltingly back to reality.

"I think there is a left turn coming up...this is the one that their website said wasn't recognised by satnav. It's called Farm Gate Road."

"I'm on it," I said, peering out of the window in search of the road.

"Can you not see it on the map?" said Charlie.

"No, I can't do maps, I don't understand them."

"Oh God," said Charlie. "Well, have a look out of the window and see whether you can see it. I'll drive really slowly.

So, we trundled along the country lanes at a ridiculously slow speed with a very, very fat lady hanging out of the window looking for the road, while clutching a map that would easily have told her where it was.

"Here, look," I said, spotting a small side road that appeared to lead up to a farm. It had a gate about 20 yards along it. "This has to be Old Farm Gate Road. It has all the ingredients."

Charlie slowed right down and looked at the road, then at the map.

"It does look like it," she conceded. "It leads to an old farm and it has a gate. What other clues could we ask for? Yay! I think we've found it."

Charlie indicated and pulled into the lane, stopping just before the gate. I rolled myself out of the car and waddled over to it, unlatching it and holding the gate open, bowing down to Charlie with a real flourish as she drove through. I got back into the car and we drove in and around the corner. As soon as we drove to the other side of the house, there was a great big flutter as hens and chickens flew up everywhere. Peacocks came striding up to the car and geese began to make the most horrific crying sound. Charlie jumped on the brake.

"Fuck," we both said, as the animals made a colossal noise, screeching and screaming and flapping all around us.

"Reverse...let's get out of here," I said.

Charlie was just sitting there. I couldn't understand it.

"Let's go," I said. "This is obviously the wrong place. This is the farmer next door. He's mentioned in the booklet...they get all their fresh produce from him."

"I know we're in the wrong place, but I can't start suddenly reversing or I'll crush half a dozen peacocks."

I looked in the mirror at the birds gathering behind us. Charlie was right...there were birds all around the car now.

"OK, look - don't panic - I'll get out and shoo them out of the way, then you reverse. OK?"

"You're going to shoo them away? What are you, all of a sudden? Some sort of champion ornithologist?

"I don't know what that is, and I've no idea how I'm going to shoo them away, but I'm willing to try. Are you ready to reverse when I give you the signal?"

"Yes," said Charlie.

"Right, OK."

I clambered out of the car and found myself ankle deep in mud. It was like thick chocolate sauce. I pulled my foot out and moved slowly to the back of the car, taking off my hoodie and waving it in the air. "Shoo, shoo, shoo," I cried. "Off you go birds, off you go. And you, peacock – be away with you. Go, go. I clapped my hands ferociously and they ran, flew and quaked away.

"OK, go," I cried and Charlie put her foot down hard on the accelerator. The car growled but didn't go anywhere. "Take the handbrake off," I instructed.

"I haven't got the handbrake on. The car is stuck. I can't move it at all. It must be because of all the mud."

"Oh God," I said.

I could see two figures in the distance, walking through the field towards us. One of the guys was waving a stick in the air. He was clearly ranting at us, presumably telling us to get off his land and to stop petrifying his birds.

"Right, strategic thinking," I said, trying to sound like I had half a clue what I was doing. I should point out at this stage that I don't drive and know nothing about cars. Still, in the absence of anyone else's advice, mine would have to do.

"OK, I'll try pushing the car," I said, wading round to the front. I now had mud all over my pale pink jogging bottoms and my beautiful new trainers were completely covered. You couldn't see what colour they were (pink in case you were wondering).

"Are you ready?"

"Yes," said Charlie, and she pushed her foot down hard on the accelerator. I pushed with all my might and mud splattered up everywhere. I could feel it in my hair and on my face. There were chickens and hens all over the place, all of them clucking and making the most terrible row. In the distance I could hear the farmer shouting. "Get out of there. What do you think you are doing? Get out of my hen coop."

Oh Christ, the car wasn't going anywhere and the angry looking men were getting closer.

"Let's try again," I suggested, with one eye on the men who were fast approaching, and the other on the peacocks who kept striding confidently behind the car.

"Are you ready?" I asked again, and I primed myself to push with every fibre of my being.

"Go," I said, and Charlie reversed the car. I pressed my whole body against the bonnet and pushed with all my might, the car skidded a little then went flying backwards and I went with it landing with a heavy thump on the ground. My lovely pink and white yoga kit now covered in mud. There was mud on my face and my hair, feathers stuck to me and chickens all around were looking at me distastefully as they clucked and ran around.

"Quickly, get in the car," said Charlie. I clambered to my feet, sliding in the mud as I attempted to run towards the car. I waddled over to the passenger side and joined her. I was filthy from head to foot; stray feathers had nestled in my mud-coated hair. I could taste mud and see it lying on my eyelashes. I'd never been so filthy in my entire life; I was caked in it.

Charlie reversed out and onto the road. She stopped for a moment so I could shut the gate. The trouble was, the men were coming, getting closer, and their voices getting louder.

"They'll shut the gate, let's just go," I said, slinking down into the seat. "Go, go, go..."

Charlie raced away from the farm as if we'd just done a bank robbery or a drugs deal.

"I don't know where to go now," she said, but a minute later, there was a very clear road sign on the right.

"Farm Gate," I shouted, and Charlie threw the car across the road and up the narrow lane, leading to Vishraam House.

We drove along in silence. It was a long, gravel drive with pretty pink flowers in pots all along it, until the driveway opened out and there, in front of us, was a magnificent country house - a lovely white building with turrets and a huge oak door. It was stunning.

"Wow," said Charlie, stopping next to the half a dozen cars parked outside. All the other cars were super expensive looking. Charlie pulled into the space in the middle of them and we stopped for a moment to admire the views.

On the right of the house there were horses and cows in the fields. On the left, near where all the cars were parked, there was a meadow full of wildflowers.

"Just look at that," I said, sweeping my mud drenched arm across to indicate the bucolic scene. There was a gorgeous lake with trees either side, lovely, colourful, plants and shrubs all around. I went on holiday to Corsica once, and this reminded me of that place - just bliss, utterly idyllic.

"I can't wait to see what the house is like," I said to Charlie.

"I bet it's amazing," she replied. "I'm so excited now. This weekend is going to be brilliant. Just one problem."

"What's that?"

"You. You're covered in mud. Just look at the state you've made of my car. You can't go into her house like that."

"I'll have to," I said. "I can try to wipe some of the mud off on a towel, but what else can I do?"

Charlie was looking down towards the lake. "You're going to have to go in there," she said.

"No way. I'll freeze to death."

"You can go in, quickly wash the mud off, and then dry yourself. You'll be in there for five minutes, and you'll be clean. What other option do you have?"

"But it will be freezing in there," I said.

"If you're really quick, you'll hardly notice it, she said.

"Hardly notice what? The freezing cold?"

"Yes - it's probably lovely and refreshing when you get in there."

"Yeah, sure," I said. "Why don't you come with me if it's so wonderful?"

"Because I'm not filthy," said Charlie. "Just go in there and wash it off. You could've cleaned yourself in the time you've been sitting here talking about it. We've got towels with us in our bags, just go and do it."

"I really don't want to," I said, looking down at the cold looking water. Yes, it was very pretty, and would look lovely in a photograph, but I didn't want to go *into* it.

"Just go," said Charlie. "You have to, or we'll have to sit here all day. You can't go in there like that."

Just as Charlie and I were debating how on earth else I would get the mud off if I didn't go into the water, the grand oak door in the middle of the house opened, and a petite, dark-haired lady with a broad smile came dancing out.

"Hello, hello, welcome, welcome," she said in what sounded like a faint Italian accent. Then she stopped in her tracks when she saw me. "Oh, my goodness, what happened to you?"

Charlie thought quickly on her feet. "Mary loves mud rambling, so went mud rambling before we came here," she said.

"Oh, how wonderful," said the lady, smiling more broadly. "I do like adventurous women. I've never heard of mud rambling but you must come on our early morning rambles, you'd love it. We end up at the top of the farmer's fields, scaling the high hills, and wading through brooks, clambering over trees and bushes... Just your type of thing I'd have thought."

"Yes, just my sort of thing," I lied.

"Great, then I will definitely organise a serious ramble for you on Sunday morning. Now – let's get you into the shower."

If I'd had any sense at all, at that point I would have got out of the car, turned, walked away and kept walking until I got back to London. But I didn't. I agreed that mud rambles were wonderful and smiled at her, completely oblivious to just how insane the weekend ahead was about to become.

CHAPTER SIX

"Hello, you're back" said the lady with the big smile and the fancy, foreign-sounding accent. "My name's Venetta. I hope the water was OK."

"It was great, thanks," I replied. "Much better than the lake would have been."

"Yes, it's very cold in there. Lovely and refreshing, but desperately cold. Much nicer to have a warm shower after a mud ramble."

"Yes, I agree completely," I said.

The shower had, indeed, been lovely. It was situated in an open-air shower block at the back of the house, near the small swimming pool. The showers were proper power showers and the water had been beautifully warm. Now I was back in the main entrance hall where Charlie had waited for me. I was wet rather than dirty and wrapped in a white dressing gown that only just about went around me. I imagined these gowns were huge on most people - making them feel swaddled, warm and safe. It barely fit me, meaning there was great danger of overexposure. With every step I took, I held the front of the gown together lest it gaped open. I didn't want our friendly host to see any of my unwaxed lady bits. I didn't want to cause alarm in this serene building in this beautiful part of the country.

"Right then...who's who?" she said, pulling out her notes and taking two sheets of paper out.

"I'm Mary, this is Charlie," I replied, putting out my hand to shake hers, but she just bowed, smiling at me, and moving her hands into a prayer position.

"There's no need to shake hands," she said. "We tend to greet each other in a simpler way."

"OK, I'll try to remember that," I said.

"You know that shaking hands is about lack of trust, don't you?" she said.

I gave her a confused look and said I didn't really know anything about that. "Yes, the handshake was developed as a way of proving to people that you weren't carrying a weapon. If they took your right hand that would show them you were unarmed."

"Oh," I said. "I didn't know that."

"Here, we don't need proof that you come in peace, we don't need proof of your character...we trust you and believe that you will do no wrong."

I had a sudden flash back to the peacocks and the hens in the farmyard, flapping their way out of the path of the car, the angry farmer charging down the hill, and the way we'd driven off without closing the gate.

"Take a seat," she said, and I looked round for a chair. There weren't any that I could see. When I looked back at her she was sitting on the floor in the lotus position. Good God.

Charlie and I clambered down onto the floor, Charlie executing the manoeuvre with much more dignity than I managed. I sat with my legs out in front of me. There was no point even pretending I could do the limb origami thing. Next, there was an awkward silence while she breathed deeply and noisily. Charlie and I glanced at one another, not knowing whether to join in, ignore her or fetch her a tissue.

"Let us rise," she said.

Christ, I was exhausted already. I clambered to my feet.

On the table in front of her were rice cakes, sausage rolls, low calorie crisps and wine... not unlike those that I'd brought with me. She indicted them and looked back at me.

"Yum," I said, raising my eyebrows and smiling. "That's cheered me up!"

"Not really 'Yum' though, is it?" said Venetta dropping her head to one side and looking at me in what you could describe as a maternal fashion or a patronising fashion, depending on your point of view. I decided to go for patronising.

"While you were in the shower, Charlie brought your bags in from the car," she said. "There was a suitcase which Charlie said belonged to you, and Jonty has taken to your room, along with Charlie's holdall, and there was also a carrier bag.

"I'm afraid that I couldn't help but notice that it was full of food and drink. I don't want to be a complete spoilsport, but you will get the most out of this low-calorie retreat if you – well – eat low calories. If you don't, I'm afraid you won't feel the benefit in your body, your mind or your spirit. Do you understand?"

I nodded like a naughty schoolgirl.

"I think it would be the best thing if I took this bag. I will give everything back to you when you leave. If you really want them, you will find them in this cupboard. But I urge you to resist taking them. I think it would do you a lot of good if you tried to stick to the programme and just live a much simpler life while you're here. I think you will really feel the benefits if you do."

Charlie and I stood there like naughty schoolgirls while she took the bag over to a cupboard and pushed it inside. "I will leave them here. They are yours to take away with you, but I think you will find that, by the end of the course, you no longer want them. This is the advanced yoga weekend with raw, vegan, no-sugar, and no salt food. Under the guidance of the Guru Aaraadhy Motee Ladakee you will find that you can cleanse and clear and direct attention to your inner self so you can focus on the yogic practices. I'm afraid that will be much harder to do if you eat sausage rolls and drink wine every night."

"Of course," I said. I looked over at Charlie. There was so much wrong with what Venetta had just said that it was hard to know where to start. She had taken our snacks - that was one bloody awful thing. Thank God I had a whole pile more in my suitcase. The other terrible, terrible thing was that we appeared to have been booked onto the advanced course with a guru.

"Peace be with you," she said, as we stood, open-mouthed. "Now, let me show you around the house - please treat it like your home. I think you will enjoy your couple of days here very much. I know you will enjoy meeting the guru...we call him Guru Motee for short. His full name is very difficult to remember. Here... look at the house..."

The place was amazing, as we knew it would be from our first glance of it from outside. We walked around behind her, listening to her sing-song voice describe the place, and I'm sure both of us were thinking the same thing - why didn't we tell her that we weren't booked on the advanced course with a guru. We were booked onto the most basic course in the brochure. But we stayed silent, and just watched as we were led around. I was embarrassed about turning up covered in mud, and embarrassed about the snacks, I didn't have the strength to admit that, in addition to all that, it now turned out we were on completely the wrong course.

Venetta took us from the wide hallway with its beautifully polished wooden floors and gorgeous antique style table through to the rooms at the back of the house. She told us that she loved antiques and regularly went on antique finding missions to London and all over Europe. It showed... the house boasted class and sophistication. Everything looked so expensive. She must have been making a lot of money from her yoga retreats and investing it in the house.

She took us first of all into the conservatory where the mindfulness and meditation classes were to be held. It had a lovely warm, cosy feeling...there were soft rugs piled up at the side of the room, comfy armchairs, and piles of mats and blankets in the far corner. Next to the conservatory was what looked much more like an exercise class room. The wooden floors, the mirrors, the bar. Everything you expect of an exercise room in a gym.

"This is where the yoga takes place," she said. We walked through that to another small room at the back where one-to-one yoga classes took place. The room had mirrors all around.

"Blimey, this is all quite intensive," I said, trying to ignore the sight of myself beaming back at me from all angles in all the mirrors.

"Well, intensity is what you expect at this level, isn't it?" she said. I glanced at Charlie as I felt myself shrink a little.

We walked out of the private tuition room and back through the main yoga room, out into the body of the house, where Venetta showed us the dining room, a small but rather richly appointed place that looked more formal than those we'd seen previously.

She opened the door and showed us the outside area where I'd had my shower, so Charlie could see the swimming pool and hot tub area. There were lots of deckchairs to relax on, and an outdoor table for when the weather permitted outdoor eating.

"We tend to eat outside in the summer whenever we can," she said. "But if it gets too cold, or it rains, we just head for the dining room."

We walked back through the front of her home, and she showed us a sitting room with a library room trailing off it. It was a lovely house. It was a shame we had to do exercise...it would be a great place to come and chill out, read books, laze around, and eat lovely big roast dinners.

"Feel free to use any of the rooms," she said. "I'd like you to treat this place like your home... borrow any of the books you want to read and let me know if there's anything I can do to help."

"Thank you," I said. I was tempted to say: "You could help by giving me back my snacks," but that felt a little unfair given how friendly and welcoming she was being, and given that - to be fair to her - we were on a detox yoga retreat and it did explicitly say in the brochure that we were not to bring any food or drink into the house, and to eat only what was provide..

Venetta wandered up the stairs, pointing out all the rooms on the first floor. We were based in the loft on the top floor, there were just two bedrooms up there. Charlie and I were sharing one of them. It was a lovely big room, very plain, with wooden floors and white bed sheets, white chest of drawers and white towels. There was a kind of wet room - a large shower at the side of the room, equipped - of course - with white soap, white shampoo and white conditioner. I don't know what it was with all the white – perhaps it was about being serene and healthy and pure or something. It was perfectly nice though, if a little plain.

"I really hope you'll be happy here," she said. "We have a full complement of people for the course today. The others are all based on the second floor, you are the only ones up here, so you should get lots of peace and quiet if you want to meditate or work on your yoga poses."

"Yes, I imagine we'll be doing a lot of that," I said, as Venetta backed away to the door, wishing us a peaceful hour.

"Please report for the introductions at 4pm," she said, as she left.

"Of course," I said, bowing stupidly and sitting down on my bed. "I hope you have a peaceful hour, too," I added.

"You're such a dick sometimes," said Charlie, and I nodded. It was hard to disagree with her.

CHAPTER SEVEN

"Welcome to Vishraam," said Venetta, opening her arms as if to indicate how welcome we all were before wafting them together again, gently caressing the air between them as she did so. Venetta moved her hands into the prayer position and bowed her head. I noticed that the others in the room were doing similarly, so I kicked Charlie in the shin and we both put our hands into the prayer position and dropped our heads in a way that we hadn't done since we were sitting cross-legged in assembly, aged seven.

"As you will all know, as elite practitioners of yoga, 'Vishraam' means 'relaxation' in Hindu. All of us here hope you will find this weekend to be the most relaxing and energising few days you have ever spent. We are experts at making sure the environments we create are full of kindness and joy. Please enjoy everything we have to offer. Treat the house as your own and welcome the hunger you feel on our low-calorie vegan diets. Enjoy the way your body responds and lift yourself to the challenge of performing yoga here. It is only by overcoming that we reach a higher place."

There were nods and murmurs from around the room and I realised that Charlie and I were the only people who'd had no idea what the Hindu for 'relaxation' was. I also realised that this was the second time that Venetta had referred to us as 'elite' and 'experts' which seemed both unusual and concerning. The only yoga I'd ever done in my life had left me face first in the pot plants at the garden centre, calling me an 'expert' in yoga would be like calling Donald Trump an expert in tweeting. No, simply not true. The opposite of 'expert' in fact.

"We're supposed to be on the bloody beginners' course," whispered Charlie.

"I know," I said to Charlie. "We *are* on the beginners' course. I don't think she realises. She's eaten too many hemp seeds or something and doesn't know what she's doing."

"I think we're on the wrong course. She can't have got it wrong twice. And look at these people – they really don't look like beginners to me."

There were eight of us on the course in total. I looked around the room at them...all looking so sincere. It troubled me how thin they all were, all of them together weighed about as much as I did. Blimey yoga people are thin. Have you seen them? All wiry and serious-looking. The guys on the course looked as fit and lean as athletes but I couldn't imagine they were much fun at parties. Or anywhere. I don't imagine they could have had a day's fun in their lives. I really hoped they'd prove me wrong.

Venetta invited us to sit round in a circle while we welcomed one another with serenity and kindness. I glanced at Charlie as Venetta said 'serenity and kindness;' and we both tried not to laugh. It wasn't that I thought what they were saying was mad or anything. Nothing wrong with serenity and who on earth could object to a bit of kindness? I suppose I was just a bit embarrassed, I'd never heard anyone talk in such an unselfconscious way before and I couldn't help but giggle.

I was trying hard to focus because I desperately wanted to change my life and be fitter, stronger and slimmer. I wanted to be like these people, especially the two incredibly beautiful women on the far side of the room, but it was difficult to adjust to all the sincerity. The two women must have been around the same age as me (I'm 30), but in all other ways they were completely different - beautiful, elegant, relaxed, composed and slim.

"This is our safe circle," said Venetta.

Everyone was sitting with their bony legs crossed into the lotus position. They were all holding their arms out, palms up, with their hands resting gently on their knees. It was hard enough for me to get myself down onto the floor, without me attempting to contort my legs into a fiendish tied up position. We all sat there in silence.

Just when I was starting to think some of the guys in the group had fallen asleep, Venetta started chanting and the others all joined in - deep sounds resonated through the room...sounds which made no sense. I sort of joined in but felt such an idiot chanting and oooing and ahhing. The loudest noise came from a very handsome man with dark hair, my God, he was good looking, like a young Elvis Presley.

Finally, it all stopped, and Venetta told us to relax. I immediately lay back and got myself as comfortable as possible, but when I looked up, the others had remained in the lotus position and were looking at Venetta who was looking quizzically at me.

I scrambled to sit up as quickly as my size would allow. "There's no need to sit up," she said warmly. "Just make yourself comfortable while we introduce ourselves."

There were six people in the group in addition to Charlie and me... a mixture of ages and both sexes were there...the one thing which united them; the one thing they had in common, was that they were super slim and super fit looking. Unlike me.

I looked over to smile at the lovely dark-haired man and caught sight of the two very beautiful women on the far side of the room. They were the gorgeous women I mentioned earlier...really, they were the most elegant looking people I have ever seen. They sat there, smiling beatifically in their coordinating leisurewear. They looked simple and comfortable but their clothing probably cost more than the average family car.

A lady who was introduced as Philippa was the slightly more attractive of the two of them. She was dressed in pale grey leggings and a matching jumper. Her clothes looked like they were made of cashmere, or some other luxurious fibre. They were complemented by a soft lilac shawl thrown across her shoulders.

Her friend wore lilac leggings and a winter white woollen tunic, with a grey shawl over her shoulders. They lounged next to one another with their matching perfect hair and teeth... Philippa's dark hair fell over her shoulders in waves...she reminded me of Meghan Markle; all dazzling smile and perfect figure. Sarah wasn't quite as beautiful as Philippa, but still had an air of wealth and good breeding about her, and the same enviable taste in knitwear. There was something very fascinating about their perfection; it seemed so complete and absolute. You just knew by looking at them that their bras and knickers matched and had been purchased from some fabulous Parisian lingerie designer. There was no way she bought them in Tesco's like I did. I could see Philippa's perfect fingernails, painted in a delicate shade of mocha, which matched her toenails.

As I watched her she lifted her dark hair into a high ponytail and tied it with a lilac band that - obviously - matched her shawl. How do people manage to do that? She looked like she was living in a magazine spread. I longed to look like her.

Sarah stretched her legs out in front of her and folded herself over them, giving me the chance to see that her manicure and pedicure also matched perfectly... In bright red which looked beautiful next to the lilac leggings. Her hair was also long, but it didn't seem quite as long as Philippa's which had cascaded over her shoulders until she tied it up. Sarah's hair was in an immaculate bun that sat high on the back of her head like a prima ballerina.

"I want to be her," I said to Charlie as Meghan Markle introduced herself. "I've been doing yoga all my life," she said. "It was something my mother introduced to me from an early age because she ran her own yoga studio."

"Of course she did," I mumbled to Charlie. "While we were eating crisps in front of Neighbours, Miss Perfect was meditating in the tree position...life's so unfair."

"So unfair," said Charlie. "But don't mention crisps...you're making me hungry. Still can't believe that woman stole our snacks."

I looked over at Charlie and we shook our heads in mutual incomprehension at the fate that had befallen our foodstuffs.

"I spend my time helping people wherever I can," said Perfect Philippa. "I also love to go for walks along the beach and I like to bathe in the ocean when the stars are out. I sit on the rocks reading poetry at night and I practice yoga every day."

It turned out that Sarah was equally well-versed in the art of yoga. She had met the gorgeous Philippa at nursery school and they'd been best friends ever since. They smiled girlishly at one another and I expected butterflies to emerge from between them and tiny cartoon deer to dance around them.

"These people are so perfect," I growled at Charlie, with undisguised jealousy.

"I reckon one night Sarah will do one downward dog too many, lose her mind and strangle Philippa to death in the middle of the night using just a pair of fashionable cashmere leggings."

"Ha!" I squealed, rather too loudly, prompting Venetta to turn and focus on me.

"Yes, you express yourself however you feel you need to," she said. "Yoga can be a moving experience, feel you can let your voice respond to it if you need to. That goes for everyone. If you want to chant or express emotion, just do that. Don't hold feelings in. Would you like to chant?"

"Who? Me?" I said.

"Yes, I wondered whether you needed to give voice to your feelings."

"No thanks."

"OK then. Why don't you tell us all your name and a little about yourself..."?

"Er...sure...there's not much to say: my name is Mary Brown and I work in a DIY and gardening centre in Cobham in Surrey."

"Try again," said Venetta. "This time don't tell us about your work. Your job is something you do to bring in money so you can live your life...tell us something about that life."

"OK, well I tend to go to pubs and restaurants and watch lots of telly with my boyfriend Ted. My favourite thing is when we go out for one of those 'eat all you can' Chinese buffets and drink loads of wine. I love that."

"OK," said Venetta, with more of a sneer than a smile. "Well, it's lovely to meet you."

The rest of the room had fallen completely silent during my speech. Now they were encouraged by Venetta to speak up, one-by-one, and explain who they were and what they did with their time. I noticed that all of them were careful not to say where they worked. Then the focus turned back to Venetta and she looked at us all.

"I know you have come here for a variety of reasons, some of you are thinking of training to be yoga teachers, others of you want a dedicated weekend of practice. But, whatever you are here for I want you to remember the fundamental principles of yoga and the importance of treating one another well, and most of all yourself, well. It's important that we love each other and love ourselves. You're not here to change your body, you are here to make your health better and that, in turn, will help to change you and make you a happier, more relaxed and able person. I want you to love your body and feel happy and whole. Only when you do that will you truly be at peace, and be able to create the body, the relationships and the life that you desire. Namaste."

"Namaste," we all said.

It was time for us to head back to our rooms for some alone time before a mindfulness course, a short unguided yoga session, and then dinner.

Charlie and I sat on our small, firm beds and looked at one another.

"I quite fancy that dark haired man," I told her.

"Diego?" she said.

"Yes. How did you remember that?"

"I'm good with names," she said. "He's good-looking, but he spent all his time staring at Philippa."

"Are you saying that Perfect Philippa is more attractive than me?" I questioned.

"No, he was probably staring at her out of sympathy."

"Probably," I agreed. "I didn't think there would be men on the course. It feels quite weird in some ways."

"Why?" asked Charlie.

"The idea of them wanting to come here and leap around in yoga gear for the weekend, eating bean shoots and sun-dried tomatoes instead of going to the football with their mates then getting hammered."

"Yeah, I guess," said Charlie. "I don't know of any men who'd do this. Would Ted ever come to a weekend of yoga?"

"God, no," I said, with a chuckle. I couldn't think of anything funnier. "He would hate it. Imagine him going to mindfulness then 'free expression' yoga."

Charlie laughed. "I can't believe you told her you like getting pissed with your mates and having huge Chinese buffets. She couldn't have looked more shocked if you'd told her you slept in a chocolate fondue."

"What was I supposed to say then? Make it up?"

"Yes – make it up. Say something impressive like that Philippa woman did. She said she liked to bathe in the ocean when the stars were out, you said you liked to shove your face full of Kung Po chicken and beef curry. She wins."

CHAPTER EIGHT

Charlie jogged and I waddled back down the stairs to join the group for the mindfulness session. "At least it'll be dinner time soon," she said to me in an attempt to calm me down. I think she could see the fear etched across my face. Watching the videos of yoga from the comfort of Charlie's sofa, and practising the odd move in the garden centre had been OK, but now we were here I was worried about whether I was going to be able to cope. Everyone else looked so different from me...so bloody fit and healthy. And mindfulness? What was mindfulness? These were things I never came across in my normal day-to-day life.

"Do you think you're allowed wine on the retreat?" she asked. "You know, with dinner,"

"You have to ask?" I said. "I imagine that the starter will be a plate of raw vegetables and the main course will be salad and new potatoes and pudding will be fruit salad and some light, calorie-low mousse."

"Surely not on the first night?" said Charlie, appalled at the thought. "They'll break us in gently, won't they?"

We wandered into the exercise room to find everyone in there, going into the cupboard to fetch big air-filled balls, mats and blankets.

"This looks alright," I said to Charlie, as we wandered in to join them. "We're going to play on space hoppers, then have a little sleep. I might be better at this yoga lark than I thought I would be."

Philippa and Sarah were already sitting on their balls...both pink. All the balls in the cupboard were green, so I could only assume that they had brought their balls with them. They had matching purple mats and light pink and pale purple blankets. I knew they were going to drive me insane with jealousy by the end of the weekend.

I collected my green ball, a rather tatty black mat and a grannyish looking blanket from the basket by the side and lay my things down to the far right of the room. Charlie positioned herself just behind me and the two men on the course set themselves up next to me.

I knew that one of the men was called Martin, he was a rather jolly-looking chap with a warm smile and open, welcoming face. He was a bigger build than most of the others there. Not fat by any means, but less skeletal. He looked as if he'd eaten sometime in the last 20 years which the others didn't. He was completely bald and had a sore-looking rash running up the side of his right leg. I decided that he'd lost his hair because of alopecia or something. Whatever it was that was afflicting him, I hoped it wasn't contagious.

"I'm looking forward to this," he said. "I don't know much about mindfulness so it'll be good to find out about it. I mean - when I say 'don't know much' - obviously I know about serenity through Buddhist chanting."

"Yes, obviously...we all know about that," I said.

"But mindfulness is an interesting idea, isn't it?"

"Yes," I said. "I don't know anything about it either."

"Well, don't worry - we'll struggle through together," he said, and I decided right there that I quite liked Martin.

Next to Martin was the very good-looking guy with the Elvis sneer. He said his name was Diego. I smiled at him, but he looked away, and didn't seem interested in talking to anyone. He just sat on his yoga ball, eyes close, humming gently to himself.

"OK, let's get started," said Venetta, entering the room in grey leggings, very similar to Philippa's, and with a shawl not to dissimilar to the one Philippa had been wearing earlier.

"Oh, you've taken your shawl off," she said to Philippa, immediately discarding hers.

Charlie kicked out at my ball to check I'd seen the exchange, and nearly kicked me off it.

"She's channelling Perfect Philippa," said Charlie with a small guffaw. "How bloody weird. Who would copy someone else's style?"

I decided not to share with her the thoughts I had about running out to buy grey leggings like Philippa's as soon as I got home.

"Yeah, weird."

"I'd like you all to sit on your ball and relax," said Venetta. "Mindfulness is about being in the here and now with no judgements and no ill feelings, it's about tuning into yourself and just existing. That is a difficult thing to do when we've all got such busy lives and so much going on, so I'm going to show you some tricks to help you do it...these simple things will help you reconnect with yourself and allow you to be present here and now. They will give you a feeling of complete relaxation and you'll feel incredibly safe and relaxed if you get it right.

"First of all, I would like you to touch the fabric of the trousers or leggings that you're wearing. Does it feel rough or smooth? Warm or cold? Feel down the seam. How does that feel. Now feel the skin on the back of your hand. How does that feel different? How does the skin on your knuckles feel different to the skin on your hand?"

Venetta went on like this for about 15 minutes, advising us to touch different things and describe them in our heads. It sounds like a completely ridiculous waste of time, but it seemed to work...I found myself completely relaxing as I focused on the simple things.

"Now touch your hair. How does that feel? What about your face? OK, now just close your eyes for a minute and think about where you are and how relaxed you are. You're safe, warm and surrounded by friends. No harm will come to you. Just relax."

By the end of it, I felt amazing. I don't know how or why it worked, but I felt great...completely relaxed and happy.

"Doesn't that feel good?" said Venetta and I nodded furiously. I was slightly light-headed, like when you've had a couple of sips of wine on an empty stomach and you just start to feel a little bit woozy and floaty...not drunk at all, just warm and lovely.

"Lots of nods, that's great to see," she said. "Remember with mindfulness that what we are trying to do is bring the focus back to the breath...the essence of life. Caring for ourselves and loving ourselves has to start from within. We need to pull our attention inside and connect to our breathing. By doing this we can keep calm and clear our mind and have a real understanding of ourselves and our body and what it is that we need from yoga to help us develop awareness and affinity. If we are not fully in the present then we aren't practising yoga, we aren't really existing, we have moved too far into our heads, not in our bodies and not in our hearts. Mindfulness can help us escape from our minds when they start the limiting chattering.

"Another way of incorporating mindfulness into your everyday life, is to stop and look at something and describe it in great detail. Look at all the intricate patterns, try to describe colours, fibres and the way the light dances off glass and marble. By doing that you put yourself into the detail of the here and now and stop wandering off into the future or worrying about the past. I think would be useful to get into pairs for this one."

Venetta pointed at me and at the very handsome Diego which was just about the best thing that had happened to me since the idea of this whole yoga lark started. "You two together," she said. I smiled warmly at him and he just stared back looking frightened.

"Once you're settled in your pairs, turn to the person next to you and describe the pattern on his or her blanket. Really look at the blanket describe the colours, the pattern, the texture... Try to completely lose yourself in it."

"Right," I said, turning to the handsome Diego. "Do you want to go first or shall I?"

He lifted a hand and pointed gently at me. He didn't seem to want to talk to me, or anyone else, at all. I wasn't convinced that was going to get him very far in this talking game, but I continued regardless.

"Okay, sure," I said. "I'll go first. Well, your blanket is kind of browns and greys mixed up together there are some black lines in it and it's sort of rough. Your turn."

I didn't know whether Diego was going to break his silence, or whether he'd taken some sort of monastic vow and was determined to remain quiet for the whole weekend.

"Your blanket is slightly rough to the touch, like touching a cow. Not soft like a cat. The colours are muted shades of earth brown, not quite chocolate, smokier than that, and a rather dull army green. It's a slightly faded-looking green, the sort of colour that an army uniform might go if it had been through a hot wash too frequently. The colours play with one another through a criss-cross pattern and the whole effect is reminiscent of an old lady wrapped up in a blanket, sitting by the fire on a cold November evening."

"Oh," I said, feeling completely outdone in the speaking game by the man who never spoke. "You've done much better than me."

"It's not a competition," he said. "We're all here to learn and grow and develop...together and as a group. There's no competition."

"Right," I said. "But you'd still have won if it had been a contest."

"No contest, no winners or losers," he said. "Just peace and light."

"Peace and light," I repeated, uncomfortable in the seriousness and sincerity in his voice.

"If everyone would like to stand up, we're now going to do some unguided, or free-wheeling yoga, just to get you limbered up and in the right frame of mind for tomorrow's activities. If it's OK with you, I was going to do a short film of the session so we can use it to show prospective guests what our opening session is like. If there is anyone who doesn't want to be in the video, and they have clicked tick box on the application form, then obviously will make sure they're not pictured in the video. I looked over at Charlie: "Did we click any tick boxes?"

"I don't think so," she replied. "I don't really know. We booked the wrong bloody course...tick boxes were the least of my concern."

It seemed unlikely that they would want me doing yoga in their video to encourage people to come on these yoga weekends in any case, so I decided not to worry about it too much... I was absolutely sure that their video would be full of images of perfect Philippa and sidekick Sarah doing majestic things in expensive knitwear.

"Okay let's start with some sun salutations then you can move into your own work," said Venetta. I wasn't entirely sure what 'my own work' was going to involve, since my whole experience of yoga to date had been limited to falling into the pot plants after trying to do the tree position at work.

We did the sun salutations and I was okay to begin with: we put our arms up in the air then

bent over to touch our toes. Philippa touched her toes, I just about managed my knees. I had very little flexibility and the small problem of a large, protruding stomach to contend with.

From toe touching, we jumped back into a plank position and dropped our stomachs on the floor (to be fair, this was easy for me, because my stomach was already almost on the floor) then went up into downward dog (basically this is shoving your bum into the air with straight legs), then we went into these lunges and back up again. It all seemed much harder than anything we had watched them do on the You Tube videos, but I still didn't think it was beyond me... I thought I could have a fair shot at doing it, but then the crucial moment came.

"Okay let's speed up to proper time now then," said Venetta, and they all started doing it at such a pace that I was struggling even to get down to touch my toes before they jumped their legs backwards and moved through the routine, I got myself in a complete mess trying to keep up with them, missing half the poses out in order to reach where they'd got to. At one stage I seem to be doing an entirely different routine to everybody else.

"Okay, let's just leave it there for a minute. Carry on doing the sun salutation if you want to, or you can do other yoga poses if you're more comfortable with those."

While the others carried on, Venetta drifted over to me and Charlie.

"Are you both okay?" she said.

"Yes," I replied. "But I'm finding it hard because I've never done yoga before."

"What you mean – never done yoga before?" said Venetta, looking horrified.

"That's what I mean," I said. "I have never done any yoga before. I've booked onto this course in order to learn, so that I could go to yoga classes at my local sports centre."

"But this is the supreme advanced class, we have Guru coming into lead yoga sessions, this is the very heights of the heights of yoga. Only the best yoga people are here," she said.

"I thought yoga wasn't competitive," I replied. And watched as she blinked wildly. "No, it's not competitive, of course not," she said.

"They will be fine," chipped in Diego from his position in downward dog. His t-shirt had ridden up to display a quite magnificent six pack and I was momentarily distracted.

"Look, I thought we'd booked the beginners class, we clearly got that wrong." I said. "We won't get in the way, we will just do what we can at the back. Is that okay?"

"Or we could leave," said Charlie. "If you think we should."

"No, let's stay," I insisted.

"No, stay," said Venetta. "But do remember that some of these advanced techniques are going to be very difficult for you."

"Will try our hardest," I said.

I looked around at Charlie to find her gazing at me open mouthed. "That was our route out of here," she said. "You just missed the exit."

"Come on let's give it a go," I said, pushing myself back into downward dog. "What's the worst that can happen?"

CHAPTER NINE

I don't think we should be here," said Charlie, when we were back in our room. "We should have sneaked out when she told us it was an advanced class. I mean - what the hell are we doing on an advanced course? It's insane."

"Yep, it's insane but we should just try to make the most of it," I said, in what I thought was a very grown up fashion. "Let's go and have dinner. I'm sure we'll both feel better when we've had a nice meal."

"Yes, OK," said Charlie, giving me the sort of dejected look that one usually associated with a little girl who's been told she has to go and visit her aunty and uncle instead of going to a party. She and I made a very basic effort to get ready. This was a casual retreat and we'd been told there was no need to get dressed up for dinner, so we were planning just to wear leisure wear and make no more effort than brushing our hair.

It was a relief to get downstairs and discover that the others had done likewise. Well, most of the others. Perfect Philippa and Sarah looked magnificent, of course, both of them in elegant maxi dresses. Philippa's was in emerald green, and she wore bright red earrings and bright red pumps. Sarah's dress was knee length and red. It was tight fitting at the top, then kicked out at the waist to form a lovely full skirt. She wore it with – you've guessed – emerald green earrings and green pumps. They were truly amazing.

Everyone else was very casual. The men seemed to be wearing exactly the same as they had worn at dinner, the women hadn't dressed up much either – like us, they'd just brushed their hair and cleaned up a bit.

"Please, take a seat," said Venetta, indicating the table laid out in the garden. It was a beautiful setting, under trellises with vines growing over them, like at an Italian villa, with the flames from the candles sending light dancing across the glasses on the table. With the pool lying to the side of us, and the silence of the evening enveloping us, it was all completely perfect. Until the food arrived.

First it was the starter...a vegetable broth with so few vegetables in it that tasted like the water you cook vegetables in. It was dreadful. Horrible stuff. Charlie and I were sitting next to two women who we hadn't talked to earlier: Margaret, who said she worked in high finance (she'd obviously forgotten the first rule of yoga club: don't mention your job), and lady called Julia who was very weak-looking and complained constantly about how ill she felt. She told us about the flu she'd just had and how she had weak lungs and a terrible immune system and she'd been in hospital five times so far this year and she was of a very delicate disposition. The two women were polar opposites, while Julia complained of her frailties, Margaret spoke at considerable lengths of her strengths. She had a first from Oxford and then went to Harvard, then she went into the City and had worked there ever since. High finance suited her because of her combative, confident nature.

"What are you doing on a yoga retreat then?" I asked. "Forgive me for saying this, but you don't seem the type to be here. You're kind of an alpha type."

"Absolutely I'm an alpha type, 100%. But my husband makes me come on these every six months or so because he says they calm me down. I like coming because I lose weight. It's like a cheap spa, really. Not that I need it to be cheap. I have plenty of money."

"Yes, I got that," I said, rather rudely, but she was annoying. So annoying.

More food came and I rubbed my hands in joy, then stopped rubbing them, because the main course was a side plate with salad on it. No protein, no bread, no anything. Sprouting mung beans and bean sprouts with lettuce and cucumber and leaves from the garden. It was dismal.

Desert was no better...three walnuts and a sliver of watermelon. And that was it. My stomach felt like it was eating itself I was so hungry.

Just as we were starting to feel like things were as bad as they could ever be, Julia gave a shriek. "Oh my God – birds," she squealed, as a dozen or so chickens came clucking into the garden.

Venetta came out and looked at them quizzically. "How did you get out?" she said, then turning to us. "The farmer must have left his gate open. All the chickens have escaped." Charlie and I dropped our heads and looked down at the ground.

"Shit," I said. "I bet that was us."

"It can't have been. That was hours ago," said Charlie.

"Perhaps the chickens have been wandering around for hours?"

Venetta called the farm, and minutes later the farmer charged into the garden with his hands on his hips. It was the same guy who'd been shouting at us earlier. He definitely locked eyes with me as he surveyed us all, and I looked quickly away. He must have known it was me who he'd seen - I was twice the size of everyone else.

We all helped to collect the chickens up. "This afternoon, someone drove into the farmyard and disturbed the birds. Does anyone know anything about that?" he asked, gruffly. "I haven't been able to calm them down since and the gate's broken."

I carried on trying to catch chickens and ignored his question. We definitely hadn't broken the gate; all I did was open it.

"If anyone knows anything about a blue car that came into the farm yard, please let me know," he added. We all nodded and said that we would. Then we helped to take his chickens out to his Land Rover. As we walked back through the car park, I glanced at Charlie's car, it was blue, and covered in mud and feathers.

"Thank God he didn't see it," I said, relieved that we'd parked it in the middle of the cars so it wasn't instantly visible.

"I know," said Charlie. "What a bloody nightmare. We'll have to sneak out and wash the car later just in case this is all our fault. Bloody feathers everywhere - look at them."

I smiled at Charlie but she looked utterly fed up.

"What's the matter?" I asked.

"I just can't cope with this little food."

"Do not fear, Mary's here," I said. "Come with me."

I led a dispirited Charlie up the stairs and told her to sit on her bed. I then lifted my suitcase onto my bed and opened the compartment that I hadn't hitherto emptied.

"When I went to the garage I bought loads of snacks," I confessed. "Some were in the bag that Venetta took, but most of them are here..."

I tipped out crisps, cakes, biscuits, chocolate and wine and I thought Charlie was going to cry with joy. "Oh my God, I love you," she said. "I mean - you're mad and everything - really batty at times, but this is amazing. Amazing."

Then she gave me the biggest hug imaginable, and we began opening wine and crisps.

CHAPTER TEN

The thing I always notice, when I eat next to someone else, is how different their attitude to food is from mine. Charlie was thrilled that I had snacks in my bag because she felt really hungry. I was thrilled that I had snacks in my bag because I love food. Charlie ate some crisps and a couple of biscuits and said 'that's better'. I wasn't like that. Once food was open in front of me I became obsessed with it. If the packets were open, I knew that nothing on earth would stop me from eating it all...my lust for food was like a wave crashing onto the shore.

Charlie sat back and poured herself a glass of wine and I continued to 'pick' at the food as we sat there. Charlie was full; I don't think I know full...it's not a concept I'm familiar with. My 'picking' in these circumstances usually results in me consuming more calories after we've eaten than I do while we're eating. I ate four biscuits to Charlie's two and had five handfuls of crisps to Charlie's two, but that was the very least of my problems around food. Because after we'd eaten our 'little snack' I continued to 'pick' and I finished the crisps, ate another packet, finished the biscuits, ate half a cake and ate a packet of pork scratchings...all during the 'picking' phase of the meal.

We finished the bottle of wine and were feeling nicely merry.

"Shall I open another one?" I said.

Charlie smiled. "Of course, but I think we should go down and wash the car first. What do you think?"

I knew we should. The farmer was bound to come back round before we left this place, and if he saw the way the car looked - covered in dried on mud and feathers, he'd know it was us, and probably make us pay for damage or something.

"Yes," I said. "Come on - let's go and do it now, then we can come back for more snacks."

It was 11pm and the house was eerily silent. Charlie and I crept down the stairs without putting the lights on, trying not to let them creak, hoping not to slip. We tiptoed into the kitchen and found two large pans and a roll of kitchen paper. We filled the pans with hot soapy water and tiptoed towards the front door. I had kitchen roll stuffed under one arm and a huge, heavy pan in my hands. I was desperately trying not to spill any of the water as we went. We got to the front door and I put down my pan and pulled the door open, as I did the most astonishing sound peeled through the house.

"Oh Christ, it's the alarm," I said. "Bollocks, how are we going to explain this?"

We stood there, in our pyjamas, carrying huge bowls of soapy water, while a man who I'd seen around the house, but who appeared to have no particular role, came running down the stairs, carrying a baseball bat. Behind him was Venetta screeching "Be careful, be careful." She was dressed in a frilly, flirty little negligée in baby pink that looked as if it belonged in the 1950s.

When the man got level with us, he stopped in his tracks.

"Did someone try to break in?" he asked.

"No," said Charlie. "We tried to break out."

"Oh, my goodness, it's you two. What are you doing?" asked Venetta, regarding the bowls of soapy water with confusion.

"Cleaning the car," said Charlie.

"At this hour?" said Venetta. "Can it not wait until tomorrow? Or when you get home?"

"No, it can't," said Charlie, looking at me for support and help.

"I've got OCD," I said. "I can't sleep unless the car is clean. It's just one of those things."

"Oh, I see," said Venetta, though she didn't really look as if she had a clue what I was on about. "OK then, well if it will help you sleep, by all means, clean the car, but you'll need better equipment than that. Jonty, can you pull the hose out for them?"

Really?" he said.

"Yes, it's OCD. We need to be supportive. You do the hose, I'll get car cleaner and brushes."

The man half sneered at me as he went outside and it struck me that he could do with coming to one of the mindfulness courses. The way he was wielding the baseball bat wasn't very 'Zen' at all.

"Here," said Venetta, handing me car cleaner and brushes. I gave her the pan of soapy water and Charlie and I walked outside.

"What? What on earth was that?" said Charlie when we were safely out of earshot. "OCD?"

"I was struggling," I said. "I didn't know what else to say. Now, come on, let's find this hose."

All of the security lights had come on outside the house; it was like the place was floodlit. I was aware that those sleeping in rooms at the front of the building must have light pouring through their windows.

"We better do this quickly," I said. "Or we're going to wake everyone up."

We found the hose, and sprayed it onto the car, brushing like mad and tipping car cleaner onto the sides and the back, where the mud was worse. We scrubbed for about 20 minutes until the car was sparkling clean and we were drenched and sweating like mad. "Come on, let's go get some snacks," I said, replacing the hose and leading the way back inside.

We put the pans back, replaced the brushes and tiptoed back up the stairs. Then I took the carrier bag of snacks she'd confiscated.

"Just in case we run out," I said to Charlie. By the time we reached the room, the security lights had gone off and the house had sunk, once again, into complete silence.

CHAPTER ELEVEN

S MACK! Morning came like a thunderclap. The sound of the alarm clock burst into the attic room. It was so loud I had to put my hands over my ears to stop my head from exploding. It felt like the whole place was shaking. Lord above, it was horrific. I sat up, switched off the alarm, and looked around me. Crisp packets and biscuit wrappers were strewn across the floor and two empty wine bottles lay next to the bed. Yep, that was why I felt so damn awful. We'd stayed up til about 3am drinking wine and laughing about my sudden-onset OCD. The alarm had gone at 5.30am. Our first yoga class of the day was at 6am.

"Up you get, Charlie," I said. "It's time for yoga."

"Good morning ladies and gentlemen, welcome to Advanced level Ashtanga," said a small, scrawny woman with short, curly blonde hair tied back into a tight ponytail. "My name is Elizabeth Hill."

There were murmurs of appreciation and delight emanating throughout the room. This was obviously a famous yoga teacher who'd been brought in to run a session for us. I hoped no one could sense the panic running through me. I glanced at Charlie; she looked as horror-stricken as I felt. At least we'd placed ourselves right at the back of the room.

Then, the madness began, as we started the class with ten sun salutations. On and on we went. I just copied copy everyone else and tried to keep out of sight. It was all going so fast that I was struggling to keep up.

I saw Venetta had come into the room. She was dressed all in black and wandered around, looking at everyone, clapping randomly and saying "Very good, very good." She said nothing to Charlie and me, of course, because we weren't very good. I kept catching sight of the two of us in the mirror...there was no disguising it...we were very bad.

Venetta stopped at the side and watched Philippa and Sarah for a while. They looked beautiful of course...Philippa was wearing cream, loose fitting shorts and a matching cream top. You could see flashes of her blue crop top underneath when she bent over. Her legs were so long and tanned, it was impossible not to stare at them. Sarah wore the same, but with a bright pink crop top underneath. They both had ponytails.

Philippa's was tied with a pink ribbon to match Sarah's crop top and Sarah's was tied with one in the same blue as Philippa's crop top.

"I think we should match our outfits like that," I whispered to Charlie who instantly stuck two fingers up at me and nearly fell out of downward dog.

"Now could we all turn to face the other way?" said Elizabeth, moving to stand next to Charlie and me.

Aahhh...no. I was at the front of the class. I stood there, facing everyone, in my baggy yellow tracksuit trousers and Daffy Duck t shirt.

"Turn around," mouthed Charlie.

I spun on my heels and we were told to repeat the sun salutations...with me at the front, and no one to copy. Nightmare. Do you know how hard it is to copy someone in a mirror? I tried to copy the people behind me by watching them in the mirror. It was awful. I was all over the place. In the end I wasn't even attempting to do sun salutations, I just moved around a bit - stretching up occasionally, touching my toes occasionally and going down into a press up position every so often.

"And... drop into child's pose," she said finally, ending my embarrassment.

Venetta had left the room while we were busy downward dogging and touching our toes. I saw her creep back in again. Rather hysterically, she was wearing white shorts and a matching white top. She looked nowhere near as elegant as Philippa and Sarah but it was clear that she was dressing like them.

I glanced at Charlie. "Did you see that?" I asked.

"Yes," she said. "The woman's bonkers."

"OK and come out of child's pose. We're going just roll from side to side. This will loosen up the spine and massage the internal organs before we go on."

I had a feeling that I was going to be good at rolling from side to side. I might play my joker on this one, I thought. We began slowly moving from side to side before we actually rolled. I had Charlie to one side of me, and Martin the other.

"OK, and roll more, go further over," she said.

Martin had managed to roll himself up the mat a little, so his bottom was in line with my head. He had on rather skimpy running shorts and I noticed that the scabby rash on his calf went all up the back of his leg. It was most unappealing. Not that I was ideally placed to go around criticising anyone else's appearance, but it really wasn't very nice. And why on earth was he wearing such tiny shorts? He looked he'd come in fancy dress as a footballer from the 1970s.

"And, have a go at rolling," said the instructor. "Just gently, roll from one side, over you go..."

I just lay there. I was enjoying the rest. I didn't plan on rolling anywhere. But as I enjoyed the short rest, Martin decided to commence rolling, he swung over, rolling his body as he'd been instructed. As he finished, there was a slapping sound, like someone had slammed half a pound of Cumberland sausages on the ground. I looked over to see that the entire contents of his shorts had escaped through one of the legs. His substantial penis and balls lay on the shiny wooden floor.

"Goodness me," he said, rolling away. "Very sorry about that."

CHAPTER TWELVE

"I feel sick," I told Charlie. "I really didn't need to see the tackle of some old, bald bloke with a serious skin infection."

"So you keep saying," she replied.

"It was disgusting. Really awful."

"Never mind, we've got the guru-led session in five minutes. That should be fun."

"If Martin's still wearing those shorts, I'm not going in," I said.

We were lying on our beds, exhausted. The morning yoga session had been followed by a long walk (Charlie ran half of it, which really annoyed me), and a swimming session, then lunch. We'd eaten our 'summer vegetable bowl', then darted upstairs for proper food (crisps and sausage rolls, though I couldn't bring myself to eat the sausage rolls after this morning's sighting).

"We should head down," said Charlie, getting to her feet and stretching out a little. I grabbed another handful of crisps and three biscuits and followed her down the stairs.

"Ladies and gentlemen, this is a special time on the course... The time when your meditation will be elevated and your yoga will be given meaning. I would like to welcome the man who has made my yoga journey so much more enlightened and joyful. Guru Aaraadhy Motee Ladakee."

We all looked up at the door as it swung open and a man walked in wearing a long orange robe. Charlie nudged me, and I knew she wanted me to joke about the madness of the whole thing, but I couldn't keep my eyes off him. He was the most magnificent looking man I had ever seen. I suppose he must be around 60, and he had longish white hair and very tanned skin. He was the sort of guy who you knew must have been devastatingly handsome when he was younger. He had a look about him that was half John The Baptist and half surfer dude. Not a common combination, I admit, but he looked as if he spent his mornings on the beach and in the waves, his bleached, tousled hair and pearly white teeth set against azure blue seas and skies. He looked as if he'd jumped off his surfboard five minutes ago. His eyes were the brightest blue I'd ever seen, set in this very handsome square face with the most amazing gentle smile. I think I fell in love with him straight away. It wasn't a sexual, come here I want to shag you, sort of love, it was more serene than that. There was something quite magnificent about him. I felt wholesome, warm and happy in his presence.

"Christ, look at the state of him," said Charlie.

"He's amazing," I said, still staring at him, transfixed by the vision before me.

"It's a pleasure to be here with you today," he said, bowing and sitting before us. He dropped so elegantly and flawlessly into the Lotus position, just a small glimpse of hairy tanned ankle as he sat and bowed over. I could only imagine how strong and flexible he was. Gosh, he was amazing.

"Om sahanaa vavatu Sahanau bhunaktu. Saha veeryam karavaa vahai. Tejasvi naa vadhee tamastu maa vidvishaa vahai. Om Shaanti Shaantihi," he chanted.

Everyone joined in. I did too. I didn't know any of the words, or the sounds they were making, but I chanted anyway.

"Follow me," he said. And he bent right over in the Lotus position so his hands were stretched right out in front of him.

I try desperately to copy what he was doing. I was nowhere near as flexible as him, but – my God – I was going to try.

He went through a series of yoga poses stopping every so often and holding them for such an unconscionable amount of time that I didn't have a hope. I decided to make up for what I couldn't do in yoga by the volume of the chats I didn't know the words to. I was well aware this was making me look stupid, and I could feel Charlie glaring at the back of my head as I wailed loudly not knowing any of the words.

He kept going for about 40 minutes, moving from position to position. I was absolutely exhausted but determined not to stop. In all the other yoga sessions I'd done so far, I had given up when I couldn't do it, and taken to doing my own thing. Now I was absolutely determined to try and impress him, so I would make sure I tried my damnedest to keep up, and to do it properly.

"Sirsasana," he said, and around me people started going into headstands. Oh, Christ on a bike. Well, I'd give it a go. I didn't know what I was doing, or how this all worked, but I put my head down and kicked my legs up and hoped to God I was doing it properly.

Turns out I wasn't.

I went flying over the top and landed with a huge slapping sound on the mat. If Martin's tackle sounded like half a pound of sausages, this sounded like a whole pig had been dropped onto the mat from a great height.

I really slammed my back onto the mat. There were gasps all around the room and Guru looked up.

"Are you okay?" he asked.

"I think so," I said.

I was far from OK. I felt winded and my back was stinging like crazy.

"Surya Namaskar everyone," he said. "While I tend to this little injured bird."

I giggled ridiculously to disguise the pain, as he leaned over and rubbed my back. I could hardly breath, my head was pounding and I felt like I was about to cry, but I didn't want to show him that. I looked up, like an injured bird might look at him and he continued to rub my back and chant gently.

The really strange thing was that I felt the pain subside. I'm not just saying this because he was really attractive or anything, I genuinely think he had healing hands. He rubbed down my back and it felt as if the pain lifted up into his hands.

"Does that feel better?" he asked

"That feels much better. How did you do that?" I asked.

"I am also a Reiki Master, I can lift the pain from you. Hopefully that will be much better now."

"Thank you," I said, clambering to my feet. I bowed and said Namaste, and told him I was fine to carry on. I wasn't but didn't want to look like a total wimp.

Despite the guru's healing hands, as soon as I moved my back and attempted to join in with sun salutations, it really hurt. I desperately wanted to make it look as if he'd magically made me better, so he'd like me, but – bloody hell – it wasn't better at all. It was really stinging. I swallowed down the pain and just carried on doing the yoga. We went from position to position and it was tortuously hard, the sweat was pouring down my face as I tried to do everything I possibly could. It was ridiculously difficult, and I definitely should've been on a beginners' course, but the lovely thing was that I did start to recognise some of the names and some of the positions and I'd worked out which ones I could do and which ones I couldn't. Because Venetta had said right at the beginning, in her introductory talk, that yoga practice was called that because it was always a practice, there were always things to work on, I knew that no one was expecting perfection. I decided in that moment that soon as I got back home, I would sign up for yoga classes, and try to be the best I could, then I would come back on one of these retreats and the group would be amazed at how much I'd improved.

We got to savasana and I collapsed, exhausted. My back was stinging like crazy, I had a terrible headache, and every part of me hurt, so I just lay back and listened to his manly, authoritative but calming voice as he talked about the power of yoga and felt like everything was going to be okay.

The next thing I knew, Charlie was shaking me.

"Where am I?" I asked.

"You're in the yoga class. You fell asleep," she said.

"Oh Christ. Where is the Guru?" I asked.

"He's gone, he told me to tell you that you did very well today and if you're back isn't better to go and see him and he will treat it some more. "

"My backs not better!" I screamed. "I need more treatment."

"What is it with the Guru?" said Charlie. "He is just an old man with long hair in a ridiculous orange dress."

I tried to sit up but my back hurt so much I could barely do it. "God that hurts," I said.

"Can you stand up?" asked Charlie, putting a hand out to help me as I scrambled onto all fours then eased myself onto my feet. "Yeah, I'm up," I said. "But bloody hell that hurt."

"Why the hell did you do a headstand?" said Charlie. "She told us not to do anything we haven't done before.

Why didn't you just go onto your knees and watch the others? That's what I did."

"I don't know," I said, dragging my mat across the room to put it away.

"Don't worry about that, I'll do it," she said, taking the mat and putting it onto the pile with the others. No one else was in the room. They had all left.

"I know exactly why you did a headstand," she said, as we left the studio and headed for the room. "You did it to try and impress him, didn't you?"

"Might have," I said, opening the door and feeling pain run all the way through my back. "Did it work? Was he impressed?"

Charlie burst out laughing. "He certainly looked shocked. I don't know about impressed."

"Fuck, it hurts," I said.

"Well you better go and find the man with the healing hands, then hadn't you?" she said, shaking her head. "If you need me I'll be upstairs drinking the last of the wine."

"Have we got any more damn yoga today?"

"Yes - we've got Bikram before dinner."

"Christ," I said. "Great Saturday night we have before us." Then I saw Venetta walking down the corridor. "Venetta, where's the guru? I want him to talk to him about something."

"Ahhh.... about your OCD?"

"No, the OCD seems better today. I wanted him to do some more reiki on my back," I said.

"I'm sorry, Mary, he's already left to go to a meditation commune for the evening," she said, apologetically. "Would you like me to look at it? Or maybe try an ice bath?"

"It's OK, I'll go for a lie down, and see him when he gets back."

"OK, see you for Bikram at 6.30pm," she said. "Do come, even if your back's sore, and just do what you can. Even if you just stretch out, it would be worth coming along."

I would go along, but only because it was another chance to see the guru.

I wandered up to the room to find Charlie lying on the bed, sipping wine out of the bottle. "Not completely getting into the philosophy of this course, are you?" I said, taking the bottle from her and having a huge gulp myself.

"Mmmm," she said. "I kind of am getting into it. I think I like the yoga, it's just that it's all too hard. I don't know what they're saying and I don't know any of the practices. Unlike you, that's made me want to stay out on the fringes a bit."

"Yes," I said. "I'm not really a stay out on the fringes sort of person."

"Nooo, really? I hadn't noticed," said Charlie. "What with the wild, loud chanting and the mad thumping headstand."

"Yeah, that really hurt. Can you take a look at my back?"

Charlie lifted up my t-shirt and almost squealed. "Bloody hell - it's bright red. It looks really sore," she said. "Wasn't the guru there to help?"

"No, he'd gone into meditation or something. I'll catch him after the next yoga class. I might just have a cool bath or something now, to try and calm it down."

"Good idea," said Charlie. "Shout if you want anything. I have pain killers here if you need them."

"I'm OK for now," I said. "I'll shout if it feels worse."

I had the bath and stepped out. It felt much worse, but nothing was going to stop me from going to the next yoga class, to see my lovely Guru man. I dried myself and styled my hair, doing my makeup perfectly. Neither Charlie nor I had worn a scrap of make up since arriving, but I wanted to look my best for the guru so I trowelled it on. I didn't care what Charlie said...I knew I looked much better with makeup. On went the foundation and powder, then more foundation, and blusher. Fake eyelashes, eyeliner...the works. I looked good, even if I said so myself. I'm just not the sort of person who looks good au naturel, not like Perfect Philippa.

I walked out into the bedroom and Charlie almost choked on the wine. "Bloody hell, where are you going?" she asked.

"Yoga," I replied. "Coming?"

"Sure," she said, following me out of the door and down the stairs to our next yoga class. "Which class is this one again? Come as a drag queen?"

CHAPTER THIRTEEN

Okay, so there were two things immediately wrong with the Bikram yoga situation. The first thing was that the Guru wasn't taking it. So, I was faced with having to do a yoga class with an absolutely agonising back, made-up to perfection, without any guru to show off to. The other disaster was that, unbeknownst to me or Charlie, Bikram was done in a very hot room. I mean VERY hot. Basically, a steam room. Christ, honestly, yoga is hard enough without adding in steam, heat or anything else unpleasant. How the hell was I going to cope with this?

We walked into the room that was right at the back of the house, tucked away, and it was like walking into hell. It was astonishingly hot...absolutely boiling. We could hardly see one another through the haze and heat.

"Does it have to be this hot?" I asked Venetta.

"Yes," she said. "Bikram yoga should be done in a room which is 40 °C. You'll love it when we get started.

It's great exercise and very good for your skin and your organs. It allows you to really stretch.

"OK," I said warily, taking my place and immediately feeling the sweat pouring off me. It was so warm that it was uncomfortable...like being in a tropical rain forest or something. You know that feeling when you're on holiday somewhere humid, and you're in your air-conditioned room feeling all lovely, then you walk outside and the heat and humidity hit you like a truck. Bang. Sweat begins to form on your brow then trickle down your back, and soon you feel absolutely soaking without having done anything. It's like the tube train in summer. You get on there and can feel the sweat running down your back, under your clothes and your hair getting damp, and you know that by the time you get to work you're going to look like you've been swimming.

The difference between the tube on a hot summer's day or a rainforest, is that no one is making you exercise there. Why would anyone do this to themselves?

We bend and stretch into a variety of poses, most of which I am familiar with now. I am a yoga queen, but I can feel my back stinging as the sweat runs down it and collects at the top of my leggings. It feels awful to be honest.

We do lots of sun salutations and I can almost get all the way through one without looking at the instructor for help, which is a good job because I can't really see the instructor, sweat is dripping into my eyes, I wipe it away. I try to do tree pose but keep falling over. When I land on the mat, there's a splash. We're all sweating so much that it's accumulating in puddles around us. It is – let's be honest – disgusting and unhygienic. There's also a really strong smell. This is what it would smell like if you poached humans. Not nice. Even the minty extract in the steam can't disguise it. It's most unpleasant.

Because we're sweating so much I feel absolutely parched; no matter how much water I drink, I feel myself gagging for more. I'm chugging it down my throat whenever I can but I'm still hellishly thirsty.

"And relax, lie back. Time for savasana."

Savasana is THE best thing in the world. Well, maybe not THE best, but certainly up there with chips and chili sauce, chicken tikka masala and chicken and black bean sauce. Oh, and chip butties, and half pounders. OK, so maybe it's not the best thing, but it's in the top ten, nestling comfortably between chip butties and pizza.

Savasana is basically lying down. It is when you relax and breathe deeply after yoga to rejuvenate the body, mind and spirit. Basically, whichever way you dramatise it, what you're doing is lying on your back and having a bit of a rest. Perfect.

We were told to rise after around five minutes of relaxation and to take it easy afterwards. Bikram yoga can be very draining...we should be kind to ourselves. Charlie and I walked out of the room, our heads spinning, completely soaked to the skin with sweat. My hair was plastered down against my skull and my clothes were drenched.

We ambled into the long corridor and back to the main house.

At the end of the corridor I could see someone waiting. As we got closer I realised it was Guru Motee.

"Hello," I said.

"Oh, my goodness, look at you, my dear," he said. "I've come to see you. Venetta said you were looking for me."

"Oh yes" I replied. "I just wanted you to check my back was OK."

"Would you like to clean up first?" he said. "Or maybe you should try and get a good night's rest, then I could treat it tomorrow after the morning walk, if it's still sore?"

"OK," I said. "Yes - good idea. I'm glad you'll be on the walk tomorrow." I smiled at him provocatively from beneath my luscious lashes, which I batted at him for extra effect. I was glad I'd done the full face of makeup now. At least I knew my face looked good, even if the rest of me didn't.

"Bye, bye," I said, as he turned to leave, bowing gracefully.

We walked back up to the room. "I think he likes me," I said.

"Who?" said Charlie.

"The gorgeous Guru. Who else? Did you see the way he looked at me just now?"

"Yep," said Charlie with a smile.

"What's so funny?" I asked.

"You'll see."

Indeed, I did see. As soon as we were back in the room, I looked in the mirror and saw the state of my face. My heavy-duty make up was all over the place...half my face was black from mascara and eye shadow and the other half a smeary mess of brown foundation and pink lipstick. I stared at the ridiculous sight for a while.

Charlie was sitting on her bed looking into the mirror on her compact. Obviously, since she hadn't worn makeup, she looked fine.

"My skin looks great," she said. "Training in all that heat and steam definitely reduces your pores. I've just splashed some water onto my skin and it's glowing."

I didn't answer Charlie. I just kept staring at myself. I wasn't glowing. I looked like Alice Cooper had been caught in the rain. I looked entirely ridiculous. Like some sort of hideously, nightmarish clown.

Charlie walked over to join me at the mirror.

"What's this?" she said, leaning in to lift something off my cheek. It was a false eyelash. One of the false eyelashes that I had been provocatively fluttering at the guru earlier.

"Look. At. Me," I said, slowly, emphasising each word. "I've been talking to the guru. Looking like this. He must think I'm insane."

"Well you are," said Charlie, rather unsupportively. "Completely insane, if you ask me."

CHAPTER FOURTEEN

There was a loud banging on the door at 5.30am. "Good morning. Happy Sunday," sang a much-too enthusiastic and upbeat Venetta.

"Urghhhh," Charlie and I moaned back.

"Downstairs in 10 minutes," she said, and we both heard her skipping off to ruin someone else's day.

"Christ, does she have to be so happy and lively," said Charlie. "I mean - every morning she's like this. I have no idea where she gets the energy from. It's quite insane. I'm not sure I even fancy this guru-led walk, to be honest."

"Oh my God - it's the guru walk!" I squealed in alarm, leaping out of bed (that's not true - I kind of rolled, and moaned as I straightened out my poor back, but 'leaping' sounds so much better). "I've been looking forward to this."

"Yeah, only because you fancy him..."

"I don't fancy him at all, I just like the idea of getting to know him better. Is that such a problem?" I asked.

"Nope. No problem at all," said Charlie, rolling back over under the duvet, trying to squeeze in a few extra minutes sleep.

It went without saying that I wanted to look amazing on this walk. It also went without saying that I was well aware that it was entirely impossible for anyone to look amazing while trudging for 10 miles in fields full of cattle. Still, I had to try. My appearance had been so dire when I'd bumped into him yesterday that I simply had to look sensational and eye catching and wonderful.

I headed for the bathroom and began the beautification process while Charlie moaned at me from her bed. "Switch the light off, it's too early for light," she said, while I smoothed on foundation and tried to do Kim Kardashian-style contouring and ultra-dynamic eyes. When I had finished, I went to the wardrobe, making a considerable amount of noise as I pulled out my favourite leggings and t-shirt, wincing as the hangers kept slipping off the rail and clattering as they hit the floor. The leggings were black and the t-shirt was bright pink. I usually wore a black tracksuit top with the outfit, but the last time I did that, my neighbour Dave told me I looked like a massive liquorice allsort so I don't wear the jacket with it anymore.

Instead I tied the black jacket around my waist. I looked in the mirror and smiled. Not bad for a 20-stone woman who was drunk out of her mind last night and only had three hours sleep...not bad at all.

"Are you ever getting up?" I asked Charlie, who grunted, threw the covers off and walked hunch-back into the bathroom. She emerged minutes later in running shorts and a t-shirt, hair tied back in a ponytail, no makeup. We looked like we were dressed for completely different events...her to run a marathon, me to audition for the role of head cheerleader.

"Shall we have a bite to eat before we go?" she suggested.

All this early morning exercise before eating anything was hard core. I found exercise difficult enough without trying to do it while starving to death. I opened my suitcase and pulled out fruit, rice cakes, biscuits and diet coke and we started munching away. Breakfast was after the run, and would no doubt comprise half a prune and a lemon pip in any case. We needed this sustenance.

We walked down the stairs and into the entrance hall which was flooded with early morning light despite the unsociable hour.

"Hello you two, lovely to see you," said Venetta. "I have some good news for you, Mary. I know how much you like mud hiking, so I have arranged for you to go hiking in the fields with the farmers this morning, instead of the guru-led walk."

Christ no. I really had to stop lying. Venetta had the impression that I was a mud hiking enthusiast with OCD. I didn't want to do hiking at the best of times, certainly not in mud, and certainly not when there was a perfect opportunity to spend time with the guru.

"Go on," said Charlie. "You know how much you adore a mud ramble."

"I do," I agreed. "But my back is so sore, I can't possibly go today, I'll just do the walk with the guru if you don't mind."

"Oh, what a shame!" said Venetta. "Let me tell the farmer then. You two head out and catch up with the others. They are waiting by the gate for everyone."

"Thanks for your support," I said to Charlie.

"I couldn't resist. It was all way too funny. You – mud hiking? With the farmer whose chickens we scared! Just brilliant."

By the time we reached the gate, the group was just leaving. Guru Motee was leading the charge.

"Hi, hello, Guru. Please wait a minute," I shouted, waddling along at top speed, trying to catch the runaway group.

"Hello there. I thought you gone on a mud ramble," he said with a gentle smile.

"No, I decided to come on this instead. I thought it would be nice to spend some time with you," I said, smiling in a lascivious way that made him recoil slightly.

"Ah, well I'm glad you could join us," he said. "Have you enjoyed the course? Besides managing to hurt your back. How is that by the way?"

"My back is still a bit sore, to be honest," I said. "Completely my fault though... I've never done a headstand before so it was probably unwise to go charging straight up into one."

"What? Never done one before?" he said.

"No. To be honest, I'm completely new to yoga."

"I see, quite a brave thing to do to come on such an advanced course then?" he said, giving me that lovely big smile again.

"Yes, less bravery and more stupidity I'm afraid," I said. "We managed to book the wrong course. I think it was my fault. When we were booking the course I jokingly added the advanced course into our basket, and I think we forgot to take it out."

"Well, at least it's been an introduction to yoga even if rather more intensive one then you would have chosen."

"Yes, it has rather. Although everything seems to have gone wrong, right from the start," I told him, just to keep the conversation going. I wanted to talk to him for as long as possible.

"Really, tell me about it..."

"Well..." I began to tell him all about how I had put on so much weight on the cruise, then we managed to get lost and had almost killed half a dozen peacocks and that's how I got covered in mud, and was about to dive into the lake when I was told to take a shower, then when I was taking a shower Venetta spotted all our goodies and hid them..."

When I look at the guru, he's absolutely crying with laughter.

"You are the most adorable, charming woman," he said. "You seem to give yourself such a hard time about your weight, but you're really a lovely person. Be kind to yourself. Relax and learn to go with the flow a bit more. I'm sure that weight will come off when you start to treat yourself much better."

"I don't know about that," I said. "I find it difficult. I love eating so much. I know it's not good for me, and I know I'm really overweight, but I love it."

"And now Venetta has taken all your snacks, so you have to eat tiny amounts."

"No, because I had loads more in my suitcase anyway," I said. "And - in any case - we pinched back our bag of goodies."

He was laughing at this stage.

"So, you been cheating and going up to your room and having snacks every evening after the tiny vegan supper?"

"Yes. Is that terrible?"

"No, it's not terrible, Mary. But learning to eat less food, and to focus on eating food that is good for you, and for the environment, is an important part of the course. The reason the food is given to you in small amounts if because is good for you to be deprived, occasionally, of what you think you need."

"I feel bad now," I said.

"No - you mustn't. I'm explaining why you have been given small portions. Don't feel bad; don't ever feel bad. One of the most important things in life is to spread joy and make people happy wherever you go. I know you have bad feelings about yourself with food, and I can feel the waves of negativity around you even as you talk about it; you must try to see your relationship with food more positively. You really are a funny, self-deprecating, warm and gentle soul. I think you will go far in this life. I think if you go to a beginners' yoga class, and learn basic yoga, you will start to feel better about your whole body and that will change your eating habits automatically without you having to force the change. Just start very gently. Stop beating yourself up, and worrying about how much you weigh, and how much you eat. Carry on being your own lovely self, and do a little bit of yoga as well, try to remember some of the mindfulness work, and if you incorporate those into your life, you will find yourself transformed. I promise you. And when we leave I'll give you my details so if you need to get in touch with me you can, and I'll help you if you need further guidance. How does that sound?"

"It sounds wonderful I said. "Thank you. There is just one more thing I need to mention."

"Oh, my goodness, what's that then?" he said.

"Well, you know I said that we went into the farmer's yard and reversed through his chickens and terrified his peacock half to death?"

"This was the occasion on which you landed face first in the mud and told Venetta you liked mud hiking?"

"That's the very time," I said.

"Well the farmer who chased after us, and who definitely saw me, is just coming to the field over there... Can you see him?"

"Ah yes, I can see him. Why are you worried?"

"Because I think he's looking for me. He half spotted me when his chickens ran in when we were having dinner but I managed to back away and hide. I'm quite conspicuous, given my size. He will definitely know it was me who was standing there in his chickens, flapping my arms to move them out of the way. And he is coming right towards us."

"So he is," said the guru, calmly.

"Well he might get cross," I said.

"Remember any of the mindfulness techniques? Relax, think about your environment. Lean over and touch that wooden fence there and feel the texture of it, try to relax and don't worry."

"How the hell is touching the fence going to help me when a mad farmer comes to kill me?" I said.

"He's not going to kill you, just be calm." In a strange way I feel safer and protected than I ever have in my life before. Just a couple of words from this man had put me completely at ease.

The farmer caught up with us and glared at me. He clearly knew that it was me who had been scaring his chickens half to death. He looked at the Guru, taking in the long orange robes and beard. "I'm sorry to interrupt you sir, but I think this lady here was in my chicken coop and I want to talk to her about the damage she did."

"Not now, not when we are at one with nature."

With that he walked on, and I walked on behind him. The farmer just stood there and watched us go. I needed to get myself an orange robe and a fake beard, they would get me out of all sorts of trouble.

Guru managed to get a bit of speed up so I couldn't get close enough to talk to him anymore, so I slowed down and ambled along at a more comfortable pace. I felt great for having spoken to him, as though I had been touched by some sort of magic, some sort of kindness, warmth and strength of purpose that made me feel happier and more confident. When I got back I would definitely do beginners' yoga, I would try to remember what they said on mindfulness and I would start to love myself a little bit more as he has suggested. For now though I had a half hour walk up a steep hill to do before I got back to be greeted by half a raisin and a quarter of a peanut or some other such delicacy. Blimey this was hard-core.

I got about half way up that hill before the feelings of love and gentleness departed. Everything hurt, the sun was quite warm, and I felt uncomfortable and horrible. I was getting tense and angry. Not with anything in particular; a couple of minutes early I'd been feeling happy and full of joy, but this whole bloody exercising thing hurt so much. My back was stinging and I wanted to be back in the house. Then it happened. I guess I was dragging my feet, and I caught my trainer on a rock, I went flying. I put my hand out to stop myself but it was no good. I landed in a heap with my ankle all twisted underneath me. I screamed out in pain and I heard Charlie shout: "My friend's hurt her ankle."

I heard the guru shout back: "Don't worry, we'll carry her back to the house. Then he ran back and saw it was me who'd fallen and not Perfect Philippa or Sarah who probably weight about eight stone each. He didn't repeat his offer to carry me, but he did help me to my feet, and he and Charlie supported me while I hobbled back in considerable pain.

Once we were there, he sat me on the grass and lit candles all around me, meditating noisily as I winced in pain.

"I think you need to go to hospital," he said, gently.

"Er, yes," said Charlie. "The candles aren't going to make her better, are they?"

I nodded pathetically. "Will you take me?" I asked the guru.

"It might be better if Charlie takes you, so I can run the yoga Nidra class after breakfast, but look - take this..."

He handed me a business card. It made me laugh that gurus had business cards, but I guess they had to earn a living like the rest of us. I glanced at it and saw that he lived in Twickenham. Twickenham!! That was so near to me.

"I'll go and get her bags," said Charlie, running into the house, while I lay back and smiled up at Guru Motee, luxuriating in all the attention...candles flickered, the guru chanted and everyone sat around looking at me. I felt as if I were the body at a wake as mourners wandered around me solemnly, and a priest in an orange robe spoke words of comfort.

CHAPTER FIFTEEN

Charlie helped me into the flat and I hobbled to the sofa, collapsing onto it, and resting my foot on a cushion. My phone was bleeping in my bag with messages from friends. I had written about the injury on Facebook in the car on the journey back. I'd even posted a picture of the x-ray department at the hospital. Actually, when I say 'written about the injury' what I actually wrote was: "Just injured myself on an advanced yoga course. The guru offered to carry me, then lit candles around me. Namaste."

It was technically true. I didn't want to say I tripped over my own feet walking up a hill because I was so drunk the night before, so I admit I made it look as if I'd hurt myself doing yoga.

Some of the responses were unnecessarily cruel.

"Carry you?" wrote Dave the guy who lives downstairs. "What's guru? A fork lift truck?"

"Good God woman, what on earth are you doing yoga for?" wrote Dawn, the famous blogger who I went on safari with a few months ago. She was the woman who got me a free cruise then didn't turn up! I ended going on the cruise by myself...and it was bloody amazing, except I ate too much.

The guys I went to Fat Club with had also left comments on Facebook. They were really kind and supportive.

"Well done you for going, but sorry to hear about the injury."

"You poor thing – let me know if you need anything."

"Well done for trying yoga!"

What lovely people. I must catch up with the fat course people again soon. I wondered whether they had had as many problems keeping the weight off as I'd had. I know we all lost weight while we were going to our weekly meetings, but it was so damn hard to keep the weight off afterwards. Perhaps we should set up another course?

Charlie appeared in the doorway with my bag, coat and the trainer from my injured foot. "There – that's everything from the car. Fancy a drink?" she asked.

"Sure, I'll have peppermint and dandelion tea please."

"Really? You know the mad cow isn't watching us any more, don't you? You don't have to drink that horse piss."

"I know that, but I fancy being as healthy as possible now... you know...to develop on everything the guru was saying."

"You're obsessed with that damn guru. And you didn't seem at all interested in being as healthy as possible when we were downing bottles of wine in the room at night," said Charlie.

"Good point, well made," I replied.

"Come on, it's 4pm, why don't we get the wine out, have a few drinks then get a takeaway later, or something?"

"Honestly, I really don't feel like it, I want to do my life differently from now on. I'm even thinking I might go on one of those courses again, you know, in a few months when I know a bit more about how it all works, when I've practised a bit more and when my ankles better and my back doesn't ache quite as much."

"You're going to book onto another yoga course that the guru is on, that's what you're going to do."

"I just found him very enlightening, that's all," I replied. "The things he said to me on the walk made me feel good. He made me feel like I can live my life differently."

"Well, if you're going to be all boring, I'm going to go home and unpack and sort myself out for work tomorrow."

"OK, I'll call you later," I said.

Charlie gave me a kiss on the cheek and told me to take care and not do too much heavy-duty yoga until my injured ankle was better.

"OK," I said. I had no plans to do any yoga, heavy-duty or otherwise...I just wanted to track down Guru Motee.

I pulled out his business card and the leaflet that had been handed out to us all at the beginning of the course. The leaflet had a small biography of the amazing Guru. He sounded even more incredible when I read it...he'd worshipped in India and all over south Asia, then had been in California for a while, as well as Bermuda where he'd met Catherine Zeta-Jones and become her spiritual guide.

"Catherine has a home in Bermuda and Guru would meet her there and work with her." The leaflet said. Bloody hell, I loved Catherine Zeta-Jones. I absolutely loved her. Guru Motee had to be in my life. Everything was pointing towards it.

The business card said that his studio was in Twickenham, and I was aware from what he'd said on our walk that he lived above the yoga studios. I looked up the address, pulled out my laptop and input the details. It was near Twickenham Green, I could picture exactly where it was. Where they played cricket in the summer, near the lovely pub that I'd been to so many times with Ted. Trouble was, how on earth was I going to get there, with my ankle all bandaged up and aching like crazy.

I picked up the phone rang Charlie. "Hello matey, it's me," I said. "I'm really sorry I was being so dull earlier, I've had a painkiller and feel much better now."

"Glad to hear it," said Charlie. "It's all very worrying when you decline the offer of a glass of wine."

"Ha ha, I'm not that bad," I said. "Do you fancy catching up later, and going for a drink?"

"Sure, yes – shall I come over to you since you are unable to move?"

"That would be great," I said. "I thought maybe we could go out to a pub we haven't been to for a while...there's quite a nice one in Twickenham near Twickenham Green."

"Twickenham? That's bloody miles away," said Charlie. "Why don't we just down a couple of bottles of wine at yours instead?"

"Because I really want to go to this pub," I said. "Please."

"Oh, go on then. Why don't I come and pick you up at seven?"

"Perfect," I said. I felt bad, of course; using my lovely friend to go and chase a lovely man, but I knew she'd understand. I'd do the same for her without batting an eyelid.

While waiting for Charlie, I did my makeup, got dressed up, and wrote a letter to Guru Motee. I planned to knock on the door, and if he wasn't in, I would push the letter through, saying I was sorry that I didn't get the chance to say goodbye, and how much help he had been to me, and I would ask whether it would be possible for me to meet up with him sometime soon.

Charlie arrived at about 10 to 7, telling me she was gagging for a glass. "It's such a pain to go over to Twickenham though," she said. "I can only have one drink when I'm driving. Let's just stay in the pub for a little while, then come back here to yours afterwards and have a proper drink. I can leave my car at yours and walk back."

"Suits me," I said, hobbling out to the car. As we approached Twickenham Green I urged Charlie to park the car on the side of the road very near to where my Guru lived. "Just here," I said. "There is no point going any closer, you can never park near the pub."

"But I can see spaces," she said. "And you can't walk. Let me drop you at the pub, then I can come back here and park if there are no spaces."

"No, I absolutely insist. Park here. I'll be fine," I said.

Charlie raised her eyebrows at me and made a funny face, before parking the car. I rolled out and waddled then hobbled to the pavement. We were parked next to number 47 and I knew the Guru lived at number 27. "See, I'm absolutely fine," I said, hobbling along beside her and counting the numbers down to we got to number 27.

"Oh! Look at this," I said. "I've just realised this is where my guru lives."

"Oh, I see, said Charlie. "Now I get it. That's why you wanted to come to this obscure pub in Twickenham. Because you want to bump into the Guru. And - by the way - when did he become 'your' Guru?"

"Shut up. I don't want to bump into him. I don't think he'll be sitting in The Three Kings in his orange robes, will he? I brought a letter with me to push through the door, so let's go and see if he's in, and if he's not I'll leave this letter there and we can head to the pub."

"OK then," said Charlie. "But I do get the feeling that this has got disaster written all over it."

We walked up to the door and I pushed lightly; it opened up to reveal the smell of incense. Someone had obviously been in there recently.

"He must be in," I said in hushed but excited tones.

We were standing in a hallway with a door ahead leading to stairs, presumably up to his apartment, and there was a door to the right of us which led into a beautiful yoga studio. I walked in and marvelled at the beauty of it. It was lovely, with flowers all around the edge, motivational posters, and beautiful soft rugs on the side. "Isn't it beautiful? Just the sort of place I'd imagine he would have."

"Yes, it is lovely," said Charlie, looking around. "Very stylish. More Philippa and Sarah's taste than the Guru's, I'd have thought."

"It's amazing," I said.

"Aren't you going to leave your letter then, so we can go to the pub?"

But I was too entranced to go rushing off.

"I really like it here. Oooo, look..."

There was another door at the back of the studio. I pushed it open. It led into a smaller, but equally lovely, meditation room.

"Don't you think it's got a really nice feeling?"

"Yes it has," said Charlie. "But we shouldn't have walked in here. He'll have a fit if he sees us."

"It's OK," I said. "He's a guru...he doesn't have 'fits'. I'll leave the letter and let's go to the pub."

I pushed the letter through the door which led up to stairs and hobbled away. In the letter I had urged him to contact me, and said I needed his spiritual guidance desperately. I know it said on the leaflet that we weren't to contact the Guru after the weekend, but he'd given me his card along with special permission to contact him, so I was sure it would be OK.

We walked into the pub and I went up to the bar to order the drinks while Charlie found us somewhere to sit, then she joined me at the bar to carry them back, with me hobbling behind her.

"I hope he liked my letter," I said.

"I'm sure he will," said Charlie. "I don't see quite what the fascination with him is though, why are you bothering to contact him?"

"I just think he's amazing, he's got this lovely aura of gentleness and calmness," I said.

"Yeah, I guess," said Charlie. "But still – I wouldn't really wanna be meeting up with him regularly, would you?"

"God yes. I think I'm in love with him," I said it jokingly and we both giggled and downed our drinks but part of me thought that I did have such a big crush on him that it wasn't far off love.

Charlie went up to the bar for our second round and my phone rang with a number that wasn't familiar.

"Hello, Mary speaking," I said, full of hope.

"Hello there," said a deep, mellifluous voice that I recognised immediately as belonging to the Guru.

"Oh, my goodness, it's so lovely to hear from you, did you get my letter?" I said.

"Yes, I did. How are you feeling now?"

"Much better thanks," I said. "Nothing's broken; just a sprain."

"I'm very pleased, Mary. Now, I can't really help you with spiritual guidance. I am working with lots of people at the moment. You need someone who can focus and spend more time on you. I suggest you practice yoga and seek fulfilment through that. I can recommend lovely yoga places in the area where you could go to. Would you like me to do that?"

"Are these places where you go?" I asked. "I'd really like to do yoga where you are." I was aware that I was sounding slightly stalkerish.

"No, I won't be there but there are lots of very good teachers who will be with you on your journey."

"But I really wanted to see you again," I said.

"You are very kind," he said. "I hope our paths cross again sometime. I must meditate now. But I wish you joy, love and happiness."

He said 'Namaste' and put the phone down, just as Charlie came back with the drinks. I noticed she had changed her mind and had a bottle of wine rather than a glass of wine and a soft drink.

"What happened to you driving home?" I said.

"Let's just get an Uber, shall we? I don't start work till 11 tomorrow, so I can get the bus back in the morning to pick up the car."

"Good decision," I said, and waited patiently while she opened the bottle and filled the glasses. "Who was that on the phone?" she asked.

"Oh, just mum and dad to check I got home safely from the retreat," I lied.

"Cheers," she said.

We finished the bottle in record speed.

"Shall we get another one?" said Charlie.

I knew it was a bad idea, we already felt half drunk, but I was also at that stage where I was too drunk to think rationally about whether it was a good idea to get another one or not, so I nodded, gave her my card, and told her to put on that. She walked up to the bar and I could see she was already staggering. Another bottle and she would be all over the place.

By 9:30pm we were on the wrong side of three bottles of wine and neither of us could really speak properly. We sat there laughing, talking nonsense and generally enjoying ourselves.

"I can't feel my hands," I said, as Charlie burst out laughing.

"Me neither," she replied. "Do you think that means that we should head home?"

"I guess," I said, staggering to my feet. We left the pub and walked outside into drizzly weather. It wasn't cold, just rainy and miserable.

"Let's go back and have another look at that yoga place," I said. "We can sit on the lovely soft rugs while we wait for the cab to come."

"We can't," said Charlie.

"Well you can wait in the rain if you want. I'm going inside." I pushed open the door and walked back into the gorgeous room with the lovely atmosphere. Charlie followed me. And we sat on the yoga mats pulled the rugs over us and promptly fell asleep.

CHAPTER SIXTEEN

It was I who woke first, blinking myself back to consciousness, and looking around in confusion, tying to work out where on earth I was. For a moment I thought I was back at Vishraam, then it came to me... blimey, we'd broken into the guru's yoga studio and fallen asleep.

"How are you feeling?"

I looked up to see the guru - MY GURU - standing there. He was wearing a short, towelling dressing gown. He looked quite delicious. I mean - old - but very attractive.

"Sorry," I said. "We fell asleep."

"Where do you live?" he asked. "Shall I get you home, or would you rather stay here?"

Oh My God. Was he inviting him to spend the night? What should I do? I loved my boyfriend Ted, and he was way older than me. But he was a guru. He was a flipping guru.

"Home would be great. Thank you," said Charlie, sitting up and running her hands through her hair. "And - sorry - we don't normally break into people's homes like this."

"That's OK, Charlie. I'll be right back," he said, and he smiled at me and left the room.

"Did you hear that? He invited me to stay the night," I said to Charlie as soon as he'd left the room. "I think he likes me."

"I'm sure he likes you, Mary, but I think what he meant was that you can stay here on the mats if you like."

"Nope, that was definitely a come on," I replied. "I think he...Oh!"

I was stopped mid-sentence by the sight of the guru walking down the stairs, accompanied by Perfect Philippa.

"Oh hello," I said. "What are you doing here?"

"I live here," she said. "We live together. He doesn't drive so I'll take you back."

"You live together?" I said, but Charlie interrupted.

"Thanks so much," she said. "A lift home would be great."

"He's way too old for her; way too old," I said, whispering to Charlie, as we walked to Philippa's car. "What's she thinking?"

"Same thing you were thinking, by the sound of it..."

We got to the car and – of course – it was one of those which bleeps when you don't plug the seatbelt in. She sat there waiting for me to click my seatbelt. "It won't go around me. They never do," I said, feeling my face sting with embarrassment.

"Would you mind trying," she said. "We can't drive all the way to Cobham with this thing bleeping."

I tried and failed.

"I'm sorry," I said, as we drove along, with the noise getting louder and louder. Eventually we reached the area in which Charlie and I both live. Philippa dropped me off first.

"Thank you," I said, as I rolled out and hobbled to the kerb.

"No problem," she said. "Just one thing; please don't turn up at my house again, or phone us or put letters through the door. OK? Guru is very peace loving, but me? Not so much. Namaste."

"Namaste," I said, as I hobbled away, looking back to see Charlie's face, wide-eyed and startled, beaming through the window. Perfect Philippa and the guru. Who'd have thought?

It was 2am by the time I got back, and I crashed out straight away. I didn't wake up until midday when Ted came bashing on my door to take me to lunch.

"How was it?" he asked, after he'd given me a big welcome home hug. I gave him the potted version and he shook his head in disbelief.

"Wherever you go, you get in trouble Mary Brown. Did you enjoy it though, despite all the minor hiccups? You know - the lack of food, getting your snacks nicked, scaring the chickens, angering the farmer, getting covered in mud, pretending to have OCD, almost breaking your back and your ankle, and being on entirely the wrong course. Despite all that - how was it?"

"The mindfulness was really good," I said. "I liked that because I felt so relaxed and warm and happy afterwards. I'll definitely do that again."

"What is it, how do you do it?" he asked.

"It sounds daft, but you just have to connect with yourself in the moment, and you do that by stopping and looking intently at things, like feeling the seat you're sitting on, and trying to describe little details."

"OK," said Ted, looking totally confused by the whole thing.

"What else did you do?"

"Well, there was this guru who came in to do yoga with us and he was excellent."

"Will you meet up with him again?"

"Na, I don't think so," I said. "I might do some beginners' yoga classes because I think it will be good for me, but I'll keep away from gurus for now."

As I spoke there was a loud knock at the door. Oh God No. Surely not the guru, or Perfect Philippa come to warn me off again. I opened the door cautiously.

It was Dave, my dishy neighbour. "This came for you," he said, handing me a letter. "It was delivered while you were away. I had to sign for it. They said it had to be delivered to you personally. They said it was very important."

"Thanks Dave," I said, opening it out of sight of Ted, just in case it was the Guru suggesting I come over to his place straight away, but it was an invitation to a funeral.

"You are invited to the funeral of Reginald Charters," it said. "You were invited as the deceased lay on his deathbed, along with five other people. No one else is invited. We would like you to try and make it."

I looked at the letter again, and at the envelope. How odd.

"What's that?" asked Ted.

"It's an invitation to a funeral," I said. "The letter says that only me and five other people have been invited."

"Whose funeral?" asked Ted, as he removed his coat.

"Well, the weird thing is, I have absolutely no idea..."

What happens when Mary goes to the funeral?

Will she know any of the other people there?

Will she find out who Reginald is?

And, most importantly, where can she get snacks late at night in this remote, Welsh village?

Read 'Adorable Fat Girl and the Mysterious Invitation' to find out...

See: www.bernicebloom.com for all the Adorable Fat Girl books

Printed in Great Britain
by Amazon

55714530R00083